THE SERGEANT AND THE KNIGHT

JANE CARVER

THE SERGEANT AND THE KNIGHT

ISBN: 979-8-88653-465-8

Published by Satin Romance
An Imprint of Melange Books, LLC
White Bear Lake, MN 55110
www.satinromance.com

Published in the United States of America.

Cover Design by Ashley Redbird Designs

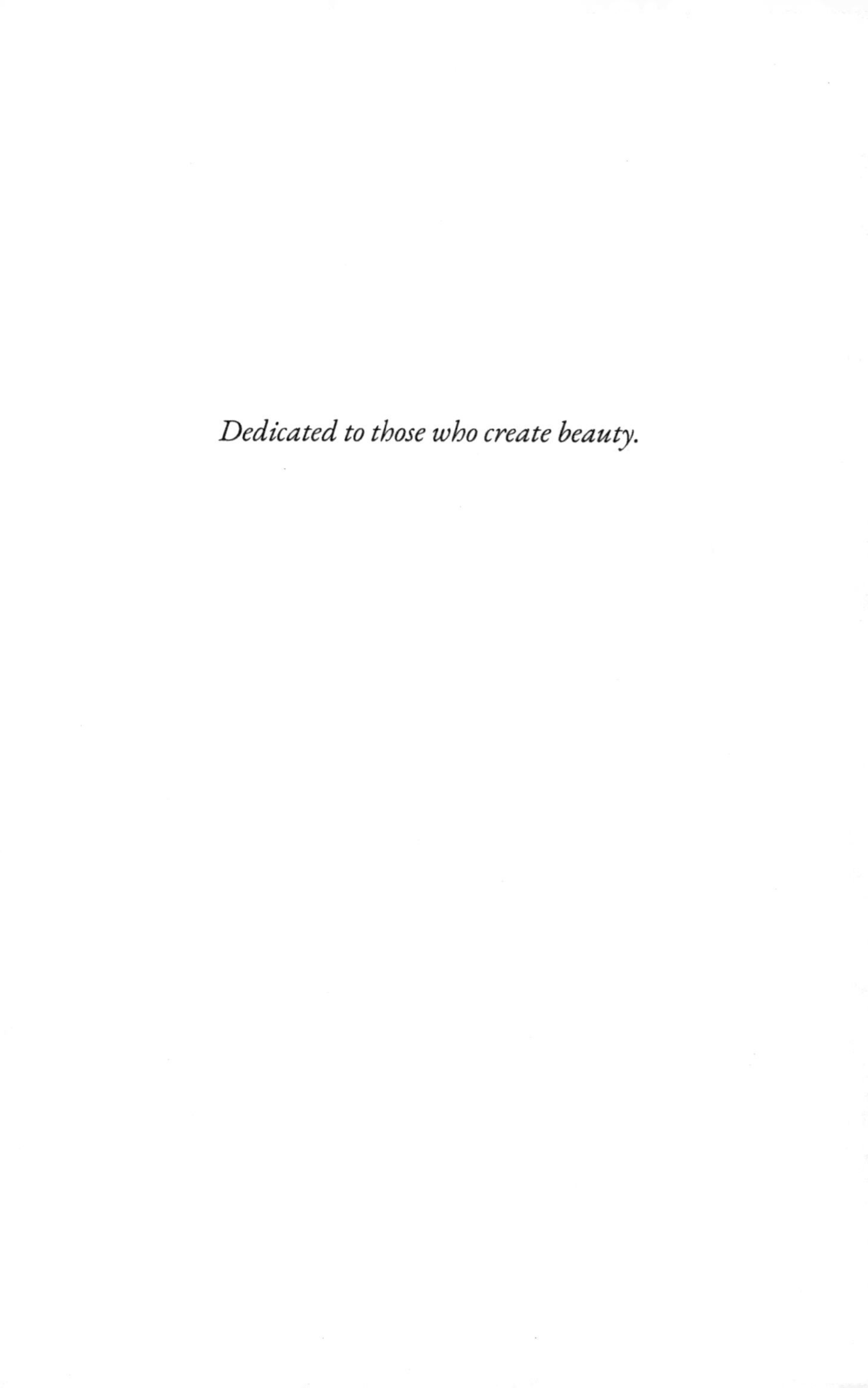

Dedicated to those who create beauty.

To begin is the most important part of any quest and by far the most courageous.

—Plato—

Foreword

What happens when you see a drawing of a knight slumped on a rock under a tree? Words start buzzing in your head if you're like me. If you have one character, you must find another. So you look for that other. And, lo and behold, once you have both, words beg to be spewed on the screen. Like a maniac, you type.

But have you ever written a complete novel ON YOUR CELL PHONE! I did! I found both pictures while sitting in my recliner in the living room. The first scene came to me so I opened the app called NOTES and used one finger to write down what was in my head as fast as possible. The next day the same thing happened while I sat in my recliner. At that point, I decided the Muse for this particular novel must have settled in that chair so that's where I wrote the entire novel. I refer to it as my Recliner Novel.

I hope you enjoy reading it as much as I did writing it. One letter at a time on a cell phone using the Notes app.

Chapter One
Not Alone

The sergeant staggered forward. At least it seemed so to him. Blood ran down his face and despite his feeble attempts to wipe it away, still flowed steadily.

Jacob Border feared he might be dying. Would die if he couldn't find his way out of these infernal woods. He stumbled, went down on one knee, his arm braced against an oak. Using the sturdy tree, he pulled himself up but leaned against the damp truck, gathering his waning breath and fading strength.

"One foot in front of the other, Jake," he mumbled, his sight narrowing to black then returning. That's what he told the men in his unit when they fought. They followed him despite his distance. He didn't want to know about their wives or kids or fears. He heard their whispers in the darkness of night or carried on the smoke of a warming campfire. He didn't want to know because he had nothing to share in return.

He'd always looked for challenges. That's what drove him forward. With no family and living on the streets of grubby towns, joining the army seemed like a reasonable challenge when he was sixteen or so.

Years later though, this war was a challenge he couldn't figure out. Why were men in the same country fighting each other? Men from the North. Men from the South. Men wearing blue uniforms. Men wearing butternut brown uniforms.

Jake stumbled again, his vision blurred. His hearing came and went. Did he hear drums? Gunfire? Was that the smell of smoke from discharged rifles? All the horrors he'd endured—and lived through—in the last three years ran together in his foggy brain.

His legs trembled now, and he fell, hitting the ground hard enough to elicit a deep groan. He reached out to a fallen log next to him but had to try several times before he actually had a firm enough grip on it. Even then, he wondered if he had strength enough to get up again.

He managed to pull himself up so his back sagged against the log. His gaze swept the area—a skill that often saved his unit from surprise attacks. He didn't trust his eyes or ears right now though.

"Maybe it's time to rest, Jake. Looks like a good place for that. Nothin' here but me and a bunch of damn trees." Saying the words aloud helped him feel alive, but he realized he wouldn't last much longer.

Jake never gave into regrets. If he made a decision that turned out bad, he took the consequences on the chin and moved on. Right now, though, he regretted not thanking the kid who beat the drums for them when they moved into battle.

A long hard day followed by a night filled with meetings with officers planning a surprise attack meant he got only a few hours of sleep last night. He woke feeling old and grumpy. He no sooner pushed back the flap of his tent and stepped out into the thickest damn fog he'd ever seen than the drummer appeared at his side, using two hands to hold a full cup of coffee.

"Real coffee, sir. Cobbed it from the captain's tent when the cook was distracted." The kid held out the cup and grinned—a grin that told the sergeant the boy created the distraction so he could snatch this cup of precious liquid.

Too busy holding the cup to his mouth then savoring the taste of actual coffee beans, Jake never got a chance to thank the boy. The youngster had no reason to bring him anything, but the kid was sharp. Must have realized Jake needed something strong to get through this next big push.

"Not dying here. I'll rot like this log." He patted the log as if it were a friendly dog then rolled over and pulled his worn-out body up onto his stomach. By dent of sheer will, the hardheaded fifty-year-old sergeant finally stood.

"You fall again, you damn fool, you're not getting up," he warned. His rational thinking played out about then. He banged from one tree trunk to the next. "I never moved like this even when I was stinkin' drunk," he told the next tree he reached for.

Too bad his next move was to a sapling not stout enough to hold his weight. The tree bent, and Jake fell face first at the base of a massive tree, its base covered with ivy.

A breeze moved over his body, cooling the aches, the insistent pounding in his head. His hands lay buried in the bright green ivy, the dirt beneath rich, refreshing. Pink flower petals lay atop the greenery. Two fingers reached for one pale petal, its softness like nothing Jake had ever felt. He held that delicate blossom as if it might break. He moved his hand, reaching for another, but the effort took more strength than he had.

His hand fell forward, resting on something hard. Not natural. Not a tree trunk. Metal? His fingers explored.

That's all he had energy for now—wiggling his fingers, using them to make sense of what he'd discovered.

A shoe? A metal shoe? His declining strength—boosted by natural curiosity—surged momentarily so he could push his fingers higher, feeling what might be an ankle. Metal still encased whatever this was. A statue? In the middle of nowhere?

He was dying—no getting round that reality any longer, but he'd be damned if he left before he uncovered what he found.

Gathering what strength he had left, he pushed his hand against the metal shoe, shoved, then screamed in excruciating pain, to lie on his back facing what he reasoned was a sight intended only for those who had finally drawn their last breath.

His arm lay propped up against a leg—one covered in plates of metal. Moveable pieces lay across the knees and elbows. Metal armor covered the body up to the head. A round helmet protected the neck and face. A cape fell from the shoulders down one side of the figure, pulled up to lie across the lap.

It sat, head down, slumped against the broad tree trunk, its hands clasped together in the lap atop the cape. Something about those hands seemed out of character. Not quite what he expected from this—this person.

Or was this a statue tucked away by some eccentric in a forgotten forest?

Person or statue, Jake recognized a warrior. Someone like himself. A warrior who gave all and succumbed to the one thing no one could defeat—death.

His arm moved so he could turn one last time. Even in death, Jake wanted to be closer. He laid his head across the foot, his hand resting on the other. Blood trickled from his head onto the metal. A hot tear trickled down his dirty cheek to drop softly on the shoe.

He thought the shoe moved, but he was dead. What did he care? His last breath came as a soft glove touched his unshaven face.

Chapter Two

This Ain't Heaven

He woke slowly, his eyes closed tightly. "Wonder what heaven's like?"

The thought quickly vanished as he realized his head still hurt. Too weak to move, too disappointed by his lack of heavenly relocation and too tired to wonder what the hell happened, he sighed deeply. His eyes still closed, he tilted his head back and gave into misery.

"Damn, I'm still alive," he muttered in a grumpy voice.

"Are you disappointed about that, Warrior, or would you prefer I finish what someone else started and send you on to the next world?"

A point of cold steel nestled delicately at Jake's throat. Curiosity along with a healthy desire to be anywhere but under that steel-tipped point warred inside the sergeant. Open his eyes and see who held that blade or let the world go and allow this person to end his life?

He settled for curiosity and a desire to meet this new challenge. Besides, if the person wanted him dead, he'd be dead by now. As he was at the moment though, he wasn't in any shape to be a threat.

Jake sucked in another breath, sighed, and resigned himself to spending the rest of this god-forsaken war in a prison camp. Flat on his back, weak as a newborn kitten, he eased his eyes open only to feel them almost pop out of his head.

Despite the blade—sword—at his throat and the fact he couldn't lift his head, he tried to scoot away from a walking metal something wearing armor from head to toe.

Toe. Shoe. Metal shoe. Jake cut a quick glance at the monster's feet. Sure enough, the shoe looked like the one he'd seen, felt.

"Death now or later when you can defend yourself?" The masked monster spoke in a low-pitched voice through a slit in the helmet.

Was that a touch of laughter he sensed? Frustrated, Jake hesitated. If he spoke with sarcasm, he might die here lying on a carpet of grass. That was his first instinct. But survival ruled his personal world. Best to say little but keep it honest. Anything else would see him dead.

"Later if that's okay with you."

The next move belonged to the metal monster hovering over him, easily holding the longest blade Jake had ever seen to his throat.

"I am uncertain what this word okay means, but I think it means you want to live." The blade withdrew. As he stepped back, he did so as if his legs were stiff. When he slipped the sword into a scabbard at his left side, he did so as if he too had suffered a long night.

Jake had no idea what to do next. He rolled his eyes but made certain the person couldn't see him do it. If Jake were healthy, he could perhaps overwhelm the guy and run. But as he was now, alive but barely, his best bet was to ride out this moment.

Metal armor clanked a few times as the man bent over a small fire, feeding in bigger pieces. Over the fire hung a carcass—a rabbit.

Dust gathered in Jake's mouth. He was so thirsty! He was starving, and that rabbit smelled so good. A thought struck him.

"Hey, am I a prisoner?" An even more important question popped into his mind. "Who the hell are you anyway?"

"I could ask you the same questions." The figure settled to the ground on the other side of the fire. Carefully he adjusted the stick holding the meat but remained silent, that round metal helmet turned in Jake's direction.

"I'm hungry and thirsty," Jake pointed out with a tiny touch of heat in his words.

"But you do not rise to refresh yourself."

Was this guy messing with him or crazy?

"I died. This ain't heaven, but I'm wondering if it ain't hell. I can't move. I want a drink and something to eat. But it ain't happening." Air fluttered his lip as he finished.

"You are warm and safe for now. This meat will finish soon, and you may eat when it cools so I won't burn my fingers or your mouth. Water flows nearby. You may have some as soon as you decide whether life is acceptable or not."

"You're making fun of me," Jake said as he turned his head away from the firelight. It was then he realized something large and soft lay over him. A cover of some kind.

Another memory—or was it a dream—flitted through Jake's mind. A cape...what he saw before he died. Damn it... before he must have passed out. Pink flowers clung to a long cape covering the monster. And now, that cape protected him from the night's misty darkness.

Little scared Jacob—Jake—Border. Not even death. He always knew his time would come. Hell, he'd lived far longer than even he imagined. But when faced with the possibility that his dream was real...that scared the bejesus out of Jake. Because he had no idea what that figure by the fire was.

Thirst woke Jake. He didn't realize he'd gone to sleep. But he'd seen many a sick man drift off to sleep in mid-sentence so great was his fatigue. Or his illness.

"I want a drink," he said, trying to see the metal figure hidden behind the fire's bright light. When he concentrated, he saw a man-like figure, legs folded, head down, knife in hand, carving. "I'm thirsty," he repeated, thinking the man might not have heard him. Jake sounded like a child with a wheedling voice.

"Let me smooth this edge," the man said without lifting his metal-covered head or stilling his hands.

Jake wanted to fidget, but the only things he could move were his fingers, toes and eyes. And his head a bit. Everything else lay like a great lump of meat. About to protest, he saw the man rise and round the fire to stand over him.

"A fresh stream flows not far from here. It helped save your life once. It will again." With those cryptic words, the man walked past Jake.

His arms and legs wouldn't obey him. He planned to run. Anywhere might be better than being watched over by a metal monster waiting for him to recover so it could kill him. His efforts to raise even his arm left Jake panting, sweat rolling down his face. His head pounded but not like it did when he died.

"Damn it! I didn't die. I'm alive. Barely," he fussed in his helplessness, a state he'd never been in before.

"You would rather be dead? This water is no longer needed then." The figure stepped back into Jake's line of sight, lifted its metal shoulders as if shrugging and stepped away.

"Wait! I didn't mean I wanted to die. I'm just thirsty. And hungry." He let his frustration show a little. "Hell, I can't even lift my own damn head." Rather than turn his face away in embarrassment, he glared with angry eyes at the other man.

"You want to live, Warrior, even if you have yet to admit it." The armored man knelt on one knee next to Jake's shoulder. "To lift your head will cause great pain. It may even reopen your head wound or one of the others," he warmed.

"For a drink of water, I'll put up with the pain," Jake spit out.

"Remember your words, Warrior, when the pain comes." With that said, the man laid his forearm on the ground next to Jake's head then eased a leather-covered hand under his head. When Jake gave no indication of discomfort, he lifted the man's head.

Pain exploded at the back of Jake's head, radiated through his body to the ends of his toes. He squeezed his eyes closed, gave a groan that came from deep within him, and felt the hand stop.

"Keep on?"

"Yes," Jake whispered through gritted teeth. Something smooth, cool, and damp touched his lips. His head came a bit higher, the pain almost shattering him, but the first sip of cool water tasted as sweet as he had imagined heaven to be. The water fell back, and Jake tried to chase it, move his head toward the most delicious thing he'd ever drank. The water returned, slipping over his lips, trickling down his scruffy cheek, a drop or two hitting his shoulder. The water fell away. The hand lowered his head. The metal man pulled back, resting against one heel, the hand holding a small cup propped on his raised knee.

"More. I want more," Jake managed to get out while fighting to keep the water down. His stomach wanted to rebel.

"No." The other man pushed up, turned and rounded the fire.

"I want another drink," Jake demanded.

"No," the man repeated calmly. But he stood, something in his gloved hand. He returned to Jake's side, ignoring his demand. "Water and rabbit. Life provides." Again, he took a knee at Jake's shoulder and held up a tiny piece of meat.

Immediately Jake snapped his mouth shut, pulled his brows together in such a deep frown it caused his head to hurt again. He leveled another hot glare toward the metal man. No one was feeding him like a damn baby.

They stared at each other, neither backing down. But the longer the silence lasted the more Jake knew two things. The other man would outlast him. And he gave the impression he might be laughing at Jake. If he didn't back down, the man might take the rabbit away.

He sucked in as deep a breath as he could muster, blew it out, twisted his mouth then nodded toward the gloved hand. The smell of roasted rabbit drifted to him, and he resigned himself to being fed by hand.

After four bits so small that Jake devoured them without really tasting them, the other man stood and returned to the far side of the fire. He sat with legs crossed, forearms on his knees while feeding wood into the flames.

"More."

"No."

"You're a hard-hearted mean bastard, you know that?" Jake wasn't getting any more to eat or drink that night, but he'd make sure the other fellow knew he wasn't happy about it.

"You have had no food or water for five days. More tonight and you will be sick. You are not strong enough to hold up your head. To spill your guts would undo your healing. I will not have it. You will sleep now."

Calm words through metal weren't what Jake would have called soothing, but they worked like magic.

A cool breeze woke Jake. The night's deep black had given way to a pale light like dawn or twilight. Across the ever-burning fire, the metal man paced, muttering, his words too low to comprehend but his tone one of aggravation.

"What's?" Jake took a second to clear his throat. "What's wrong?" His gaze swept the trees for the first time. He could see to each side without numbing head pain and straight down his body.

Odd-looking trees. Must be that infernal forest where he got lost, separated from his men and the battle. What would his commanding officer think of him? The metal man said he'd been ill many days. Would the captain think he deserted?

Worry set in. When he recovered his strength, he'd return. Explain. Maybe drag the metal man back with him to prove he hadn't run away. But then, he doubted a man like the one pacing yonder would go willingly into an army camp and vouch for him.

The other man stopped, put both hands at his waist and studied the thick canopy of trees overhead. He stomped further into the trees. Had he left Jake unprotected?

Jake scoffed. "Unprotected? Worried? Damn right, you fool, because you're too weak to lift a biscuit or take a piss.

All that's keeping you safe is a clanking walking talking bucket of metal," he said with a sour tone.

"You speak the truth, Warrior. I am indeed all that keeps you alive." The man had circled the camp while Jake talked to himself and apparently came close enough in time to hear what he said. A faint chuckle escaped from beneath the helmet.

"Pretty pleased with yourself, aren't you. I'm stuck here with you and have no idea who you are or where we are."

Words built up in his mind—things he'd thought about during the few times he was awake. "And I'm not a damn warrior!"

"You are a warrior," came a calm reply that set Jake's teeth on edge.

"I'm nothing but a sergeant in an army in the middle of a god-damn war that makes no sense. I'll probably be executed for desertion when I get back."

"Would a lord execute a warrior for doing his duty?"

"I don't know about the Lord. I ain't been in church any time recent." He squirmed a little but said no more.

"Your lord—the one to whom you owe allegiance?"

"Oh, you mean like my captain?"

"A captain, yes. He would not kill a warrior such as yourself who has served and has scars to prove it?" The man sat down between Jake and the fire.

"If the captain thought I was a coward and ran from battle then yeah, he might kill me. As an example to others." Another cool breeze passed over Jake, and he shivered involuntarily.

"You're cold. I will pull the cover higher." The man moved, one hand out to lift the cape, but Jake yelled at him.

"Wait!" His fingers, those curious fingers that found this creature—made a shocking discovery. "I ain't got no clothes on but my drawers! Why am I practically nekid?" He tried to edge away from the out-stretched hand, confusion and suspicion in his eyes, tone and mind.

The metal man sat on one hip, a knee raised, his forearm draped over the metal curve of that knee. Giving his own gusty sigh, he held up a hand, palm out to Jake. "You are cold, thirsty and hungry?" he asked quietly without moving.

Nothing like bringing up the mention of vittles to a man on the mend. Jake had to decide if he was more concerned about his lack of clothing or his next meal. Hoping he could have both the meal and his clothes, he frowned but admitted, "I could stand to eat more than those scraps you gave me last night and a few drops of water. But what happened to my clothes?"

"First food and water then I will tell you the story about how we came to be. Agreed?"

Jake simply nodded but jerked his head to one side as the man pulled the cover up under his chin before he stood. On the other side of the fire, he retrieved a small cup. Off he went.

So that was what he was carving—a cup for water. "Hope he lets me drink my fill this time," Jake grumbled.

"A bit more this time but not as much as you desire," came the other man's comment as he squatted beside Jake.

"I talk too much," Jake lamented aloud.

"Perhaps, but it proves you are healing, if slower than I would like." The man looked around. "This is a strange place. I cannot leave your side for long in order to find food. Alone you are easy prey."

With those uneasy words, the two repeated the drinking of the night before, the pain still there but perhaps not as bad. Maybe because Jake knew to expect it.

"More."

"No."

"Ain't no one ever said that to me then just walked away," Jake threatened.

"There is a first time for all things, Warrior. Recover your strength, and if I tell you *no* then you are welcome to try stopping me from walking away." The man laid down the cup, reached over and pulled a slightly larger cup onto his lap. He lifted a piece of meat so small that Jake wasn't sure he had anything between his fingers.

Only a few seconds passed before Jake opened his mouth, and the man laid the meat on his tongue. This time he chewed slowly. Without salt, the meat tasted gamey, but it was food, and he intended to enjoy it. The bastard next to him wasn't going to give him very much so might as well make the most of what he could get.

As he chewed, he heard what sounded like another chuckle, echoing hollow-like from the helmet. "You making fun of me...again?" He cut his eyes sideways at the man even as he slipped another small piece into Jake's mouth.

"Perhaps," the other admitted. "You speak of dying yet you make an effort to live. I suspect we share a common feeling—we should not be here. Yet we are. You savor your food and drink now, knowing you will not receive all you want. You value loyalty. As do I. You value honor. As do I. You value honesty. As do I, but I confess I have secrets. A few I regret. Most I do not. If we abide together long enough, you may learn one or two. I am a warrior. You are a warrior. Yet we are nothing alike."

Blowing a raspberry sound out of fluttering lips, Jake snorted, "That's the most I've heard you say." The other man held up another piece of meat, but Jake shook his head. "Ain't hungry no more, but I could use another sip of water." The man traded cups and leaned over Jake, gently lifting his head, patiently letting him drink a few more drops than last time.

Jake closed his eyes, an odd sort of comfort and contentment settling over him. "I want to rest a bit," he told the man without opening his eyes.

"A wise man knows what he wants. And when to do something about it. Pleasant dreams, Warrior."

"Yeah, and tomorrow my clothes and that story you promised me." He yawned and did a feeble wiggle, getting more comfortable.

"As you wish, fellow Warrior. It is a worthy tale."

Chapter Three
Slow Recovery

He might have eaten little and sipped only drops of water, but sometime in the early morning as the forest creatures started stirring, Jake knew he was in trouble. And the only one who could help was that other fellow.

"Hey." Jake called softly to the man who lay in full armor on his back, not far from the fire. The man did not stir. "Must be that helmet keeps him from hearin' me." His stomach rumbled loud enough he figured an army could hear it. "Hey, you! I gotta..." Holy Hell, how does a man ask for help to take a shit and a piss? If no one helped him soon, this cape would be a mess. "Hey, I need help to take a shit!" he bellowed loudly and groaned when the effort aggravated not only his aching head but some kind of wound along his ribs.

The metal man suddenly rolled to one knee, his sword in hand. "Warrior, is there trouble?" From his pose as he stood, anyone could see he searched for an adversary.

"Look, man, this isn't easy for me, and it's gonna be embarrassing for you, but that food and water I had..." Jake's words trailed off.

"Your body comes alive. You want something, and you

ask. Wise man. We shall endure." Cold morning metal clanked a few times as the man came to Jake's side. "This is going to hurt. I am sorry for the pain you will suffer." That said, he eased the covers off Jake and, slipping an arm behind his back, helped him sit up for the first time.

Black spots swam before Jake's eyes, and bile rose to the base of his throat as chilled morning air played over his skin. "Give me a minute," he asked, but he needed to relieve himself and despite pain or a sick stomach, he needed to get moving. Nodding to the other, they managed to get him standing. His legs wobbled and threatened to buckle.

"Courage, Warrior. This you can endure. This you can conquer," came a deep quiet whisper as strong arms supported Jake.

"Yeah, let's get this over." He sagged, but the arms held strong. "One foot in front of the other, Jake," he chanted as the two moved away from camp and the stream and into thick brush.

The other man, almost as tall as Jake, drew Jake's arm over his shoulder and pulled out his sword. "I will do what I can to help, but your protection comes first."

Fortune favored the two. A heavy branch lay inside the tangled underbrush. One of the twisted limbs had come down with the branch. It offered a perfect place for Jake to sit and lean against the limb.

"I can hang my ass off this. Shit that way and piss the other. Can't ask for more." He joked to cover his embarrassment, but his humor also covered the incredible pain his chest and head endured. Other than being weak, his legs apparently received no injuries though he had no idea he'd suffered more than a head wound.

"Call when you are finished." The man reached down and pulled up a large handful of sweet-smelling grass. "Grass for that ass. So my cape will not be fouled."

Though he tried not to, the man's words tickled Jake, and laughter came, bringing pain across his chest. Despite that, it felt good to laugh again. He wasn't normally a serious man. He enjoyed a joke and a good story. Wrapped up in the misery of his pains and the strange person with him, until that moment he'd found nothing humorous in the entire situation.

Eventually the two returned to camp. The metal man headed for Jake's bed, but he had other ideas.

"That log over there near where you sit. Prop me up so I can clear my head."

"That is not wise."

"Wise or not, damn it. I wanna sit up and look around. And I want my clothes." He heard the other man sniff in disagreement. "You promised, and I can't go round in my drawers. Besides, you said you'd tell me what's going on, and I figure I better be sittin' up to hear it."

"I must check your wounds first. This moving around may have opened some stitches." The man eased Jake down so his back rested against a log with thick, rough bark.

The man gathered the cape, a pair of boots that sat a foot beyond Jake's head where he'd laid and a pile of things Jake recognized as his clothes. They'd been tucked under his head all this time, keeping his head wound off the ground. The man returned with his collection but laid them a good ten feet away.

"Why'd you leave 'em there?" Sitting in nothing but a thin pair of knee-length flannel drawers allowed a chill to rattle up Jake's backside.

"If I give you your garments, you will cover yourself and refuse to let me attend to your wounds." Arms crossed over a thick metal chest plate, the man stood with feet planted firmly, the very picture of a parent out-waiting a fractious child.

"Okay. Okay. Check the wounds. Then can I get dressed?" The concession was just this side of being sarcastic.

And the other man knew it. "I washed the clothes you wore. I will not return them if one of your wounds is bleeding." Hands fell to hips, the man waited.

"Damn, you sound like somebody's mother," Jake mumbled just loud enough for other ears to hear.

"Thank you," the metal man said then knelt down by Jake. "You suffered a severe head wound. I thought you would die." He hesitated but continued as if reluctant to make the admission. "I did not want a warrior to die alone." He leaned Jake to the left, "Something round pierced your side here and here." He rose and moved to the other side, pushing Jake this way and that. Hands still covered in the softest leather touched him along the sides, checked his right shoulder front and back then reached down to lower one side of his drawers.

"Hey, what're you doing?" Jake grabbed the string that drew the flannel closed around his hips.

"You have not felt this one?" The man looked Jake in the face through his thick helmet but laid a gentle hand on a tender spot that ran along his hipbone.

Surprised he had a wound there, he studied the reddish flesh. "Is this okay? It's red." He turned worried eyes to the other.

"Move your hand, and let me check." Seeing great hesitation, he bowed his head to Jake. "Let me look. I will not lie to you."

Reluctantly Jake let go of the string and allowed the other to pull the flannel further down. A touch here. A pinch there. Discomfort but not intolerable pain. Delicately the man pulled up the flannel and tightened the string to secure the garment at the waist. "That one heals nicely. The red may be because you leaned against that branch and rubbed it." The man stood and backed up several feet. "I believe you will live, Warrior, and fulfill your destiny.

Jake guarded his tongue this time. That was a damn odd thing to say. *Fulfill your destiny.* The only thing he saw ahead was more army life though once he'd dreamed of other things.

"I doubt my life will be long enough to fulfill any destiny. The army might have other plans for me, and the fellers on the other side of this war damn sure don't want me to get out of it alive."

A pile of clothes fell into his lap. "Hey, no need to be huffy." He started separating the pieces, checking them for wear, considering the few days before he wound up here involved furious fighting with barely time to take a piss, much less tidy up.

He laid out his shirt across his lap. The thing was a dingy cotton that pulled on over his head. At the moment, he wasn't sure he had the strength to raise his arms and pull it down over his chest. Each piece was clean, something they weren't when he stumbled through that damn forest.

The other man sat on a fallen branch a ways from Jake and the fire. Something like a shield stood propped against the branch nearby. He sat with arms crossed over his chest, legs outstretched and crossed at the ankles. He sat watching. Alone. Forgotten.

"Thank you." Jake looked over at him and nodded. "I owe you. My life. My safety. My clothes." He held them up adding, "They're clean." He put them up to his nose and inhaled as deeply as he could. "They smell fresh." He hung his head and admitted, "Nothing that good's happened to me in a long time." He fidgeted for a few seconds. "Thanks."

And there they sat, staring at each other until the metal man broke the weird silence. "With those wounds healing and pulling the skin, you will suffer pain if you try to don that tunic alone." The man still sat, cross-armed and -legged, apparently waiting for Jake to ask for help.

One hand rubbed his bare chest as he gave in. "You're probably right. No need to open wounds that are healing." He fluffed the shirt over his lap a second or two. "Besides I'm puny as a baby bird and will probably fall over trying to dress myself." That was as close as he'd come to admitting he needed help.

"A wise man wants. A wise man asks. You appear to be a wise man indeed, Warrior." The other man chuckled as he uncrossed himself and helped Jake dress.

Despite his effort to stay awake after a few bites of food and half a cup of water, Jake's head nodded several times then his chin fell to his chest.

He woke with an aching back. His groan attracted the other's attention. He waved the man off but couldn't get comfortable.

"May I offer a word?"

"Sure. You're probably going to anyway." The sore back put Jake in a sour mood. Waiting for the other's advice, he looked up to see the man sitting quietly across from him. A piece of wood was shaping into another cup.

"Well?"

The man remained silent.

Jake lifted his eyes, frustrated by this metal man. But his words might have come across as mean sounding. He knew nothing about this stranger. So far, the man had been nothing but good to him. He knew he was wrong in speaking rudely.

"I'm sorry. I...my back hurts. The bark bit into it pretty good while I was sleeping. Maybe...could be you might know something that would help?" He fussed with the corner of his shirt, his worn coat no longer the deep blue it was years ago when issued. He watched the other, hoping he hadn't destroyed whatever this was between them.

The man laid aside the wood and knife, only to prop up one knee and rest a gloved hand over it. "Would not your back feel better if you laid your surcoat between you and the log? My cape will keep you warm as it has these many days."

"Surcoat?" Jake tugged on his jacket. "You mean this?"

The other simply nodded.

It took little thought or time for Jake to realize the suggestion made sense. He attempted to sit up straighter so he could slip the coat off his shoulders. His injured right shoulder didn't move well enough for him to get the coat off. The garment lay bunched between his body and the log. He tried to turn and pull it away so he could fold it neatly then place it against his back for padding. Due to the injuries along his sides though, twisting side to side wasn't working. He worked up a sweat and colored the air with a few curses before he leaned back, closed his eyes and panted like a winded racehorse.

Slitting his eyes open, he saw the metal man still reclining with wrist propped on knee.

"You got anything to say about the mess I just made of this?" He waved his hand around and tugged on one corner of his coat that stuck out from under his hip. The man across from him said nothing. The man's silence hit Jake the wrong way. "Yes, I need help. Damn it." Still the man sat.

"Yelling ain't gonna get it, is it?" He dropped his chin onto his chest and heaved a sigh. All he'd done was piss off the guy who'd saved his life, set his head to pounding again and all his injuries to aching.

"Holy Hell, I'm a jackass."

"The first sensible thing you've said these past minutes,"

the man said as he stood. He gathered the two bowls, one with water and the other with rabbit. Then he held them up, gesturing with them to Jake.

"Please, yes. I'm worn out. Something to eat and a drink would be welcomed." His long legs stretched out in front of him. His shirt was twisted around his chest and his coat lay in a tangled heap at the back of his hips. He'd made a mess of trying to prove he was getting better.

The other one sat down at Jake's side, facing him, that weathered helmet still in place. Inscrutable. When the man lifted the cup of water, Jake stopped him. Taking the cup into his own, he passed it to his left hand, leaned forward enough that he could drink without help and too much pain. He noticed though that the small cup was only half-full so he took several small sips. That way it would last until he finished eating. The larger cup only held a few pieces of meat, same as always.

"Trying to starve me to death?" he said as he took a piece from the cup. The man sat with legs crossed and forearms resting on his knees. For the first time he saw that the other wasn't eating. He held out a piece. "Ain't you hungry?" Another thought hit him. "When *do* you eat?"

"I eat when I am hungry. Enjoy what you have. I must hunt tomorrow. But I am reluctant to leave you." The man pushed Jake's hand away, guiding it back to the one with injuries.

"I'll be all right. You'll be quick." Jake finished the meat and savored the last few sips of water. "Thanks. That hit the spot."

"Like many things you have said, I do not understand these words, but if the food pleased you then I am glad." The man gathered the bowls, turning to toss a handful of sand into the bigger one, scrubbing it around then brushing out the dirt and grease.

"At least we clean our dishes alike," Jake said with a grin and a bit of movement. Which reminded him of the log and that rough bark. "Uh, using my coat as padding is a good idea. I could use a hand getting it in place."

Without another word, the two arranged the coat so it protected Jake's back. The man reached over, pulled the heavy cape up and spread it over Jake so that the cooler night breezes wouldn't set back his healing.

More wood went into the fire. This night both sat on the same side maybe two feet apart. The wood crackled as the heat hit it. Animal sounds perked then quietened. The never-ending twilight that passed for daylight slipped into the complete black of night.

Chapter Four
Jake's Story

"You promised to tell me how we got here—wherever here is," Jake prompted, his gaze resting on the fire rather than the man beside him.

"True but my tale—our story—must begin with you. What do you recall of the days before you awoke here?" The other sat in his usual position, legs crossed, hands carving on that new cup.

"Well, we fought for two days. Hard fighting. Loud. Guns and cannons boomin' all the time. Men shouting orders. Men screamin' for help. Calvary horses screamin', dying in the bombardments. We only got a few hours of sleep because we posted so many guards. Those who weren't on duty were too tense to sleep." Lost in his recollections, Jake tossed his hands around, using them to indicate positions. The firelight was the canvas on which he presented his story.

"That last morning I'd had two hours of sleep. I didn't really sleep. Too wound up. The company's drummer boy brought me a cup of real coffee. I never tasted anything better," he paused as he remembered. "Until I took those first few sips of water you brought me when I woke up.

Heaven's own water, I remember thinking." He chuckled at that comparison.

"Somewhere in the damn fog, the smoke, and the noise I got hit. Must have been more than once though I never felt these." He laid a hand on his side. "But my head..." He wagged a finger at his companion. "That I do remember. A cannon went off near me. Something flew up and hit me so hard I went down. I almost drowned in the mud in that field." He stopped, the low pounding that came and went in his head made more painful with the telling.

"When I managed to get myself out of the mud, the field was quiet though I could hear gunfire and shouting far off in the distance. The fog from that morning never lifted. I must have wandered further than I thought. I remember..." Jake's memories of his wandering weren't as sharp as those from the battles.

"My head was bleedin' pretty bad. I sort of staggered from tree to tree, trying to hook up with my men. But I fell a lot, and each time I tried to stand up...it was...harder and... harder." He stopped and swallowed. "I was about played out. Dying maybe. Maybe not. Maybe just tuckered out. I remember I fell and landed face down in this ivy sort of plant. Pretty pink petals lay on top of that green stuff, like the petals fell from a tree. My hand...found a hard boot. I don't know why, but I wanted to be near it if I were dying. I passed out after that and woke up with you standing over me."

He turned to the other man. "Not to cause offense or anything, but the sight of you scared the crap out of me. I mean, I thought I'd died. I didn't, but I thought I did." He settled his hands across his stomach under the cape and watched flames dance delicately on slow breezes.

"You did die, Warrior."

"No, I thought so, but I just passed out from losing so

much blood." Jake nodded his head, convinced dying had nothing to do with the present circumstances.

"You died. I was there. I saw your last breath."

Jake turned startled eyes on his companion but for once was at a loss for words—sarcastic, shocked or otherwise.

"I awoke at the touch of your hand on my boot. Your blood flowed freely on the metal. A tear watered the boot as well." It was the man's turn to speak to the fire. "My hand reached for my sword, but I stopped when I saw how grievous were your injuries. I leaned forward and watched as you drew a breath, let it out but did not bring in another. I waited many heartbeats, knowing you were gone. To die alone is one thing. To die so near another and not receive comfort in your passing is not right. I reached down, wanting to wish you safe passage to the next world. I touched your face, and you gasped so deeply I wondered that you did not push out what blood remained in your body. You died. But you lived again. I dragged you to this clearing for safety." The man laid the knife and cup aside then tossed the shavings into the fire.

"By the time I found the stream and gathered wood for a fire, a fever had struck you. Between the fire ravaging your body and the head wound I had little hope you would survive the night." The man tossed the last shaving into the fire and drew up one knee, clasping his hands around the curved metal guard. "I washed your body all night, but the fever was fierce. All day I wiped sweat from you. Late in the second night, the fever broke, leaving you lying in sweat. It was then I slept. Only to find you shivering some time later. You spoke many times in your fever of places you liked, men you admired. Battles you've fought. Scars you carry to this day. But you never talked of family or a loved one." The man shook himself, paused then continued. "I washed the fever from your body with the help of that cold stream," he paused to nod toward the water.

"Now I had to find a way to warm you. Over and over you mumbled, 'I'm cold. I'm cold.' I built up the fire to an inferno, pulled you closer to it, wrapped you tighter in my cape and laid behind you, your back to my front. For two days, I held you as your teeth chattered and your very bones shook. Two days ago, you fell into a deep still sleep. Were you alive, or had you died yet again? I rose to check and found you merely sleeping. Like you, I laid down and slept a long time. After some time, you seemed to sleep as any tired man would. I knew you would live but realized you would need water and food. I had nothing to give so I hunted then carved the little cups."

The man surged up and looked down at Jake. "Here we are." Heat stirred in his words, low, anxious. "Where? I do not know. When? I do not know. What comes next," the man gestured out to the night, "I do not know. But we must face tomorrow together because you and I...are all we have."

With a little less help than the day before, Jake made it through his basic needs and a meal. By mid-afternoon, he fidgeted. "Ain't nothin' to do," he mumbled.

"When the day comes that you can walk on your own, you will need to defend yourself. Perhaps you can spend time now preparing for that day. I think you will not be leaning against that tree much longer." The man sat not far from Jake, his sword across his lap, a whetstone smoothing the edge. "I sense the days around this fire growing shorter. You will return to your life—this Great War—and I..." The man sent the stone down the blade's edge with something that resembled rage."

"What will you do when we part company?" Jake felt funny saying that. In this new life to which the other man said he was born, all he'd known was safety and care at the hands of this stranger. One whose face he had yet to see.

"I have a quest to fulfill. My destiny, you might say," said the man, once more sending the stone along the blade in furious strokes.

"You keep at your blade like that, you won't have much of it left. I can almost see sparks fly when you rub it," Jake commented casually. Carefully. Without knowing this person on a deeper level, what he said might set the fellow off, and that early sword point at the throat might turn into something worse.

A sigh from inside the helmet rushed out long and loud. The man stopped, rested his hands on the blade then proceeded to reset it in the sheath and slip the whetstone into a small bag at his waist. "You are correct, Warrior."

"So this destiny? You need that sword good and sharp for it, huh?"

The man sat silent so long that Jake figured he'd crossed some line.

"Again, you are correct. You will look for many men to join. I will seek one. You may live through your war. I will not live through mine, but I will not die alone," he said in bitter dark tones. The man stood, cut a long gaze at Jake then moved silently into the thick forest.

"Damn, I ain't seen anyone that angry in a long time." Jake whistled in awe.

Jake managed to sit on the tree trunk. His side hurt, and his right shoulder was of little use. His head hurt but didn't pound. "Let's see if I can walk any. Metal man sure will be surprised to see me up and moving." One hand on the wide stump, Jake eased up, knowing he suffered no injuries to his legs. They'll work fine he convinced himself.

Through a sheen of sweat and with gritted teeth and heavy breathing, he finally managed to get his feet planted and stand. "Whoa!" His sight started going in and out, a roaring set up in his ears, and his legs started wobbling like uneven table legs. "This ain't as easy as I thought," he muttered as he swayed.

He was missing something. This wild feeling of imbalance he'd not experienced before. He needed... To be honest he wasn't sure what he needed, but his world was tilting rapidly.

"Don't be a fool! Sit down!" came a deep growl at his elbow.

Though the other man never touched him, Jake's world seemed to steady. He held out one hand in order to feel the stump as he allowed his weak knees to bend so he could sit. He wasn't graceful as he thumped onto the tree truck, but his rear end was down, steady and safe.

"That was not wise. You are no fool. Do not act like one. If you fall, it will be me taking care of you again. You are not a youthling." The man stood with hands crossed over his chest, that unmoving helmet facing him. "You know better." The man was angry.

Angry? Jake heard something else in the words. Or maybe he imagined he heard words of worry. A sense of caring. "I'm sorry. I thought I was strong enough. I didn't mean to worry you none." He honestly thought the other would deny the worry.

Instead, the man acted like he hadn't heard Jake's words. "Food will be ready soon." He reached down to the ground next to Jake. He came up with a stout straight limb maybe seven feet long. He must have dropped it there when he saw

Jake about to topple over. "Your hands want something to do. You may use one of my knives to shape this. Clean it. Put a point on one end. It should be long enough to drive back an attacker. If that fails, it should be stout enough to be used as a staff for hand-to-hand combat." He held it out to Jake. When he took it, the man reached down and pulled a short knife from his boot. He flipped it from hilt to blade and offered it to Jake.

"Thanks." Now he had a mission. A way to defend himself. A way to show the metal man he wasn't useless despite being called a warrior.

Jake worked two days with the thick branch, cleaning off the bark and shaping the ends. Despite his desire to work efficiently and quickly, his strength gave out on occasion, and he'd lay the wood across his lap and the knife by his side. Each hour that passed helped him feel less an invalid though his daytime toil meant he slept soundly each night.

Each day he stood and walked a step. By the third day, his staff was finished. He'd managed to move slowly around the fire to return to sit on the stump.

The man would sit on that nearby log, ankles and arms crossed, watching. With each success, he gave Jake praise. A few words that meant more to Jake than he would admit.

The next morning, Jake rolled to his side, groaned just a little and wished he could lie under the woolen cape longer. He finally turned to face the ever-burning fire.

Metal clanked a bit in cool mornings, he'd noticed.

A hand came down, and a voice commanded, "Rise, Warrior, and let us begin this day." Rolling his eyes, Jake let the man pull him up, less effort on the man's part and more on Jake's.

"You heal better each day. Soon we can find a path out of this godforsaken place."

"Yeah," Jake agreed, but something about moving on didn't seem as necessary as he once thought. His thoughts went round and round as they moved at his pace into the thicket.

Jake veered off to take care of his needs but found the man waiting for him where they'd parted.

"The stream is that way," the man pointed to their right. "If I leave you there, can you return to camp without help?"

That was unexpected. Jake shot the man a surprised glance. "You going somewhere?"

"Should I stay?" The man held some thin branches to one side and let Jake step to the edge of a stream, its sides soft with grass, its waters clear. "I thought you might want to bathe. The water refreshes tired bones."

Jake shot him another glance, both brows high, his eyes wide. "Uh...you've had a bath?" He cut his glance between the man and the water that bubbled with a cheery note over a few rocks as it passed the two.

"One of those secrets I kept that I never regretted was cleaning my body as often as possible. Those around me thought such should be reserved for spring and high church holidays." The man snorted. "Wearing one's helmet helps diminish the smell of others." The man pointedly let his gaze take in Jake from head to foot and back up.

Jake blushed. He'd spent so much time in his sweat that he was used to it. He refused to take a visible sniff of himself.

"I suppose I can make it back to camp by myself." He wasn't sure if he remembered the exact way, but he figured he could always follow the smell of the wood smoke.

He wasn't sure if he could take off his shirt alone though. "If you could help with my shirt?" His shoulder wouldn't let his right arm go up over his head yet. His clothes probably smelled as bad as he did. He should wash them too, but he had nothing else to wear while they dried near the fire. He fiddled with the edge of his coat, his gaze on that water, the other forgotten.

Forgotten but still there. "Fresh clothes would be welcomed as well. Perhaps I can offer my cape so you may stay warm while they dry?"

"That's jus' weird. I was just thinking about washing my things." He spoke, still looking at the water. "Sorry." He turned back to the other. "The cape. That's a good idea. Thank you." He fidgeted a second, a nervous thought flitting through his mind. To his surprise, the other seemed to read his mind. Again.

"Fear not, Warrior. I will not look." The man turned and walked away but not before he tossed back over his shoulder, "Besides I've already seen all of you." Light laughter followed the man through the brush.

Warring between wanting the man to return quickly so he could get the stinkin' shirt off and wondering what the man meant with his laughter, Jake jumped when the other pushed through the brush, laid the cape on the verge of the stream and held out both hands. When Jake hesitated, the man reminded him of the shirt.

Nervous, Jake let his jacket slip off his shoulders then turned to the other for help lifting his shirt up his back then pulling it over his head. Together they got the shirt off.

The man handed it to him and made to leave, but he turned back with hands on his hips. "You do not take teasing easily, do you? You worry I will attack you in your bath." The man gave the first real laugh since they met. "Bathe in peace, Warrior, knowing I..." The man suddenly sobered. "Knowing I will never hurt you."

Thankful the cape was generous, the two sat side by side, Jake cleaning out the larger bowl then passing both to the other.

"You feel better?" the man asked as he tossed wood chips into the fire.

"When you go day by day from one battle to another you don't have time to eat or sleep. You piss when you can. Things like that," he said, gesturing to the other man. "To be clean and not hungry or worn out. That's a dream." He picked a blade of grass, positioned it between his thumbs and blew over the edge. He created a whistling sound. He grinned and tossed the grass aside. "Little things like that get forgotten. A bath is like that. You forget how it makes you feel." He hitched the cape higher around his shoulders, set the cowl a bit higher on his wet hair. He checked that the garment covered his body, those places a fellow didn't expose except to a woman.

"Better then?"

"Yeah. Thanks." A sigh of contentment eased from Jake. He could have sworn one came from the other. "We've been here a long time. You told me how we came to be together. I told you what I remembered before..." Jake swallowed but admitted finally, "I died. But you've never said a word about how you came to be sittin' by that tree. Hell, I never told you my name, and I don't recall you ever tellin' yours. Damnation, I don't know shit about you. What you're called or even what you look like. You're a walkin' talkin' body of metal!"

He calmed, aware such frustration might not relieve his curiosity. He wanted information, revelations but then again maybe not. "I'm damned confused about this whole mess," he worried aloud as he gestured to the total darkness beyond the firelight.

"I admit I have not been honest with you. I did not

realize this would worry you so. I am sorry for that." The man sat with his hands in his lap, his head hung low. "I find...comfort...in your company in a place where we are both strangers. But such cannot continue. We must leave and find our way back to where we belong. Let us abide here one more full day then I shall share my story, perhaps to my detriment. That you must decide. We go together, or we part ways. That too will be your decision. I will abide by your word." Now it was the other man who fidgeted.

"I'm not sure I understood all you said." Jake motioned to the man. "I heard the words all right, but a lot of it makes no sense. We could just grow roots and stay here—wherever the hell this is. You promised your side of the story. I can wait. I'll get stronger so I don't hold us back. But I have to say, you abiding by what I say makes no sense."

"My tale is a strange one, Warrior. You may not like it. I hope you are the kind of man though who might understand."

"While we wait for your side of all this, can you at least tell me your name?"

If it were possible for the man's head to hang lower, as if in shame, his head dropped even lower, the metal across his shoulders rounded inward as if he were hiding. "I have no name. It was taken from me." So saying, the man stood, walked to the other side of the fire and laid down on his side, his helmet turned away from the fire and Jake.

Together they visited the stream. The man pointed out things he'd observed about the forest.

"Damn odd trees," Jake noted as he leaned his head back. "I can't even see the sky. Like living inside all the time.

Light through a window. But never the clear sky. I've never seen such a place."

"Nor have I," the other agreed, one hand on a hip, the other on the sword's hilt. "Noises at night are not known to me. I see no animals during the day except those that resemble a rabbit."

"Yeah, but you gotta admit even those look strange." Jake motioned toward a thicket, and they explored further from camp than the metal man said he'd been before.

Jake's strength definitely wasn't at his best yet. He lagged behind a few steps, pretending a closer examination of things around him.

"Let us eat and rest, prepare for what lies ahead tomorrow," the man said and turned, headed back to camp. He moved easily at Jake's side as if strolling rather than stepping out as he had earlier.

"You can go on ahead. I'll be there shortly," Jake offered, gesturing forward. He was slow to pick up on it at first, but then it dawned on him that his companion was matching his pace to Jake's. And he was walking pretty slow. He should be embarrassed but found the company pleasant. "Go on if you want," he offered again.

"The day is pleasant but as odd as all the others. I am content as I am." The man never looked at Jake, just kept moving along easy-like.

Once back at camp, the man slipped a thick stick through a carcass and sat in order to attend the cooking. Jake wandered, tired but not ready to settle. He wasn't wearing metal armor so figured the other man rested when he could.

Rounding a tree not far from camp he stopped and leaned back in order to think. But his heel struck something soft that clanked. Looking down at the base of the tree, he pushed aside leaves that covered a leather satchel. "What the hell?" Curious, he tucked it under his jacket and made his way back to camp.

His companion was gone, along with the water cup. Taking advantage of this solitary moment, Jake dropped down beside the tree truck and prepared to open the straps holding the bag closed. Maybe this belonged to someone they'd yet to meet. Maybe someone passed this way and lost it or forgot it. Excitement rose as he undid one strap and reached for the other.

A steel point—the end of a familiar sword—pressed deeply into the side of his neck. This was no warning. This time the blade bit with intention.

"Put...it...down. Now." Calm words. Deadly words.

The sword pressed hard enough that Jake moved his head away, but the blade followed. He raised one hand in surrender and used the other to drop the bag at arm's length to his side. Both hands in the air now, Jake held his breath as the metal man stood, breathing hard, the armor over his chest rising and falling deeply. The hand that held the weapon, however, never flinched or moved.

"Never again," the man whispered low. Moving deliberately, he stepped over to the satchel, picked it up without taking his eyes off Jake then slung the long leather strap over his head so the bag hung on his right side.

Stepping back and back, seeing no threat from Jake, the man slid the sword into its sheath. Without turning his back on Jake, he returned to the fire. His gaze vibrated between the roasting carcass and Jake.

Many minutes passed before Jake's heart stopped pounding. What the hell just happened? He'd found something that belonged to the other man. That was pretty damn obvious. But why such a reaction? Like the satchel held things the man didn't want him to see. All the man had to do was say it was his, and Jake would have handed it over. He figured he'd crossed some kind of line, and things were different now. But how? And why?

"We should have water to drink." The man on the other side of the fire raised his head as he spoke and lifted one hand that held the cup. "You know the way." The wooden cup sailed through the air.

Jake caught it by reflex and the fact that he'd been watching the man like a hawk to gauge what he might do next. Obviously *next* meant a trip to the stream.

The last meal of the day passed in silence. Jake refused to act differently. If the other fellow wanted to be standoffish then he'd make the move. He sat next to the man same as always. Though the other didn't eat or drink in his presence, Jake now wondered what the man was hiding. Maybe that's what he meant about letting Jake decide what would come next after the tale had been told.

Too keyed up to sleep, wondering now who the metal man was and what would happen next, Jake sat long after the other rolled to one side and slept. How does one sleep in armor, in a helmet? Jake scratched his cheek, the thick whiskers making his skin itch.

Tomorrow might be a grand day. It could also be a bad day. As Jake rubbed his cheek, he decided the day would be a fresh start so he'd better be prepared. He stood as quietly as possible, picked up his staff and stuffed the knife the other man let him keep into his boot. He'd do this as fast as possible but try not to cut his own throat. He hated leaving the other guy alone but knew he was better off than Jake with the fire nearby and his armor.

Scraping off a thick growth of whiskers wasn't easy. He had no soap to help soften the hair. He sat crossed legged at the edge of the water, a little downstream from where they got water to drink. He'd cleaned up both cheeks when the back of his neck began to tingle—from experience, a sure sign of trouble. Immediately, however, he also heard a faint grind of metal brushing against metal. He continued shaving.

The metal man walked as quietly as possible into the clearing, paused a few minutes then sat down next to Jake. All without talking. He picked pieces of grass and tossed them into the water, watching the slender lines of green float away. He found a stone at the water's edge and tossed it in the water. He never spoke or looked at Jake.

With one last scrape along his neck above his Adam's apple, Jake leaned forward and washed the blade. Using the tail of his shirt, he dried it completely including the fancy scrolls along the handle. Flipping it handle to blade, he offered it back to the man. But the other shook his head so Jake placed it back in his boot.

Rather than worry more about the next day, at least feeling if not looking better, Jake eased up and returned to camp. The man followed several steps behind. Jake didn't worry about the man being at his back, maybe stabbing him from behind. If that mystery man covered head to toe in metal armor carrying a sword longer than Jake's long legs wanted him dead then he'd be dead.

Chapter Five
Abide

Breaking camp the next morning involved nothing more than making sure the fire was completely out. They'd agreed to let it die down. That was a risk as fire might have kept them safe all this time, but they only had two small cups to carry water to douse the fire. Better it die on its own.

"That's the last of it," Jake said as he swirled a stick through the wet ashes. "I saw fire hit a stand of trees once. Cannon fire started it. Wasn't pretty watching men run from the flames that raced through there." He used a hand against his knee to push himself up. "You've got what you started with," nodding at the armor and sword which the man carried in his right hand. "I've got a...you call it a staff with one damn sharp end. Guess I'm better off than when I got here."

"You are alive, Warrior. I would say that makes you far better than when you arrived," the man said without looking at Jake.

"Never thought about it like that. Guess you're right." He moved to stand next to his companion.

The man was in warrior mode, helmet turning from side

to side, left hand carrying the shield, that long-ass sword held firmly in the right.

"We have one last thing to do before we move out. I'm damn sure not traveling with a stranger not one mile," Jake reminded his companion.

"You may change your mind. I expect you to," came cryptic words from the metal man. Though he didn't lower his sword, he sighed as if resigned to a fate that Jake alone would decide. "Follow me to where this tale began." He headed toward a particularly thick stand of trees.

Though the area was clear of underbrush, the treetops were so thick the light more resembled twilight. The man pointed to an oak, its base maybe five feet wide. Large rough-cut boulders lay scattered around its base. Delicate plants grew taller than Jake around the trunk. Pale pink flowers bloomed along the branches. Around the tree and boulders grew a dense carpet of deep green ivy. Pink petals floated down in the occasional breeze to adorn the greenery.

"Hey, this is where I found you." Jake held his staff as he moved to the large stones, touching one. "You...you sat there." He pointed to a good-sized rock. He pulled back, remembering what the other said. How he died at this man's feet then came alive again.

"Indeed," the man agreed before sliding the sword into its sheath. Turning to Jake, the man asked, "What year was this great battle in which you were so grievously wounded?"

"Let me think a minute." Jake scratched his head and tried counting days, but he'd lost track of how many days they'd been together. All he could remember for sure was spring. "It's spring, April, I think?"

"But what year?" the other insisted.

"Uh, 1865. Why?"

The man staggered as if hit broadside. He stumbled to finally rest on the very rock where Jake found him. "More than eight hundred years...eight..." The man gasped, his head shaking side to side, a slight tremor in his hands.

Shock? The man's behavior worried Jake. He'd seen men face unbelievable tasks and react this way. Surely knowing the year wouldn't have done this? He moved to the rock next to the man, his worry turning to fear when he saw the armor move as if the man shivered uncontrollably.

"What's wrong?" He reached out and laid a hand carefully on the other's left arm, aware that shock sometimes made a man strike first and injury others before reality returned. "Tell me," he asked, his deep voice as soothing as he could make it.

"Eight hundred years, Warrior. I sat at this spot for over eight hundred years," the man said softly as if unable to believe.

At that, Jake eased off the rock and took several steps away from the distraught man. Eight days made some kind of sense. But eight hundred years? That was impossible. Maybe the man was ill, imagining things. He kept a close watch in case the other attacked him.

The man sat with head down now, hands clasped in his lap. His long cape hung down his back, falling onto the ivy and petals. "I am alone, Warrior." The man had given up.

The tone of voice...despair, lighter perhaps. The hands. What was it about the hands? Rather than lay his hands atop his legs or entwine the fingers, he sat with one hand cupped into the other, smooth, curved.

Silence filled the glen. The man sat slumped on the rock. Jake stood, undecided. What should he do now?

He eased back to the rock, giving the man time to gather himself. Taking a chance that the other had calmed down, prepared to jump away, if necessary, he asked, "Tell me why eight hundred years is so important. Please," he added quietly.

"Your name. I must find some anchor in this new world."

The words he knew, the meaning Jake didn't. Still the man was calmer so he went along with the fellow's request. "My name's Jacob Border. Friends call me Jake."

"Jacob," the other repeated. "A strong name. One worthy of a warrior. This shorter name—this is more familiar to you?" The man had yet to look at Jake directly.

Maybe he's figuring out something. "Jake's just easier to say, I guess. Never gave it any thought to be honest." He shrugged, not sure where this name thing was going.

"You have fine names. No one can take them from you, can they?"

"Uh, I don't guess. Like give me a new name, you mean?"

"No." The man finally turned his helmet to face Jake. "Take your name and leave you with nothing. No way to claim yourself. And now after eight hundred years, no way to win back my name." The man shook himself and straightened. He cut his gaze back to Jake. "I have worried you. Perhaps caused great fear." The man shrugged as well. "Though you do not strike me, Jake Border, as a man who fears much in your world."

"I never gave that much thought either," Jake admitted, his staff now resting comfortably across his lap.

The other man sighed deeply. "My tale may scare you, Warrior. You must be brave for it is a tale of dishonor and magic. I can explain it no other way. You have been braver than any man I have ever known. But I broke a sacred code, was found out and punished. No name. I no longer have people or lands. I am broken. I am alone."

"No. No you're not." Jake shook his head vigorously. "We're here. Together. We'll find a way back to people. We can come up with a name for you. We can locate your family. Let them know you got lost." His attempt to cheer the other one sobered a little. "Even if you've been gone a long time." He gazed out over the glen, a little embarrassed at his words.

"Let us begin with the hardest part, Jake. You will be angry, and that is my fault. My life, it seems, has turned into one falsehood after another."

As Jake watched, the man raised hands to his helmet, undid a clasp that held a hinge together then slowly lifted the helmet off his head. Lowering the round head piece, eyes the color of storm clouds faced Jake in a face as delicate as the pink petals. Long dark lashes shaded those gray eyes. A blush sent high color into a face.

"You're a..." Jake's mouth hung open, his eyes so wide they almost popped out of his head. He used one shaking hand to wipe his mouth though it had gone dry. "You're a..." His mind was having trouble changing the image he'd fashioned of this man...this person...into that of a woman with smooth skin, pale lips, dark brows and hair a rich brown pulled back at the nape of the neck.

"You may say it aloud, Warrior. Be brave," she encouraged in a dejected voice.

"You're a woman." Once more Jake drew his hand across his face. How had he missed this? The hands! That should have told him something wasn't right. A man doesn't sit with his hands like that. But a woman would. Sudden anger filled him.

"You lied to me! You let me think you were a man!" He bound off the rock to pace back and forth in front of her. "You...you tricked me!" He wasn't even sure why he was so mad. He sputtered and mumbled, gesturing at her as he paced. The louder he got, the more forlorn the woman became.

Finally, he ran out of steam, leaving him abused and

confused. When she motioned to the rock beside her, he gave up, too muddled by her revelations.

"I find no fault in your anger, Jake."

His name sounded odd coming from her. They had never needed to address each other. They worked smoothly together as if their minds thought alike.

The woman sat with her helmet in her lap, one arm draped over it. "Now that you know this much about me, let me explain a few things about our time together. Then I will try," she lifted her shoulder and cocked her head to one side, "to explain why eight hundred years upset me so. May I?"

Afraid he might say something rude, Jake nodded.

"I never bathed in that stream. I let you think that as I let you think me a man. I have been long away from my life, in a strange place now with a strange man. I did not know you, and when I did, it was too late. The pattern of our lives was established. I merely wiped the parts of me I could reach with water. In my time, I cannot don nor remove this armor without help. I knew not if I could trust you. I trusted before and was betrayed. I couldn't take that chance."

"You telling me you've been in that armor since we met?"

She nodded but added with a touch of humor, "If we go on together, perhaps you can loosen some straps so I may truly bathe. I will tolerate no attempt to carouse as others thought to do," she informed him. She softened her words with a faint smile, the first she'd given so far.

"No, ma'am, no funny business," Jake cut his hand down, indicating his words were truthful. "What *are* you? This armor? The sword?"

"I am a knight, sir. Upholding a code to protect my liege lord's lands and people. That was my privilege and...my downfall." She gave Jake time to think about that.

"Tell me your tale, ma'am."

"I know not what that word is."

"What? Oh...ma'am?"

"Truly."

"It means...well, it's..." Jake tossed his hand up in frustration. "It's what we call a lady before we know her well enough to use her name." He cut a shy glance at her that she saw. "It would be easier if I knew *your* name," he hinted.

"I have no name. I have said this before." She refused to be disturbed by his request.

"Okay, I'll stop talking so you can." He crossed his arms over his chest, prepared to hear her story.

She nodded, accepting the task. This time she did twine her fingers, her gaze in the distance. The very far distance.

"I was born in the year of our Lord 983. By my thinking, I was forty-two when my life stopped."

"You died? Like I did? Then came alive again?" Jake was having a hard time with the year and age numbers. "You sure look mighty young," he blurted out, realized what he said and snapped his mouth shut. In an embarrassed huff, he frowned deeply, crossed his arms again and shot her a mean look, to find her grinning at him. He snorted as the heat of a blush colored his skin from neck to hairline. He pulled out one hand and made a silent rolling gesture, indicating she should continue.

She cleared her throat, without laughing aloud. "I have sat on this rock for over eight hundred years, frozen in time because I wanted more than an ordinary woman should. My father trained me as if I were a son. Trained me to be a knight. I learned quickly through hard lessons. My mother had no say. My father wanted a son. She never gave him one. So he trained what he had...me. We lived far from my liege lord's castle. We never trained where others could see for both Father and I were breaking the law."

She turned to Jake and propped one metal boot on a

smaller rock between them. "Just as you worried about being executed for being away from your army, Father and I would have been executed for breaking the Knights Code of Honor. Not because I was unprepared for battle or unable to defend myself or others but simply because I am a woman. Is this the way in your time?"

"Yes, ma..." Better not to call this knight *ma'am*. "Women follow the army. Most cook and clean our clothes, and well..." He rubbed his chin and colored a bit. "They comfort men." He felt the heat of a blush warm his skin again, but he added, "Our women don't fight in battle though."

"They are both camp followers and doxies, you mean," she clarified.

All Jake did was nod. He wasn't going to add more to that particular conversation.

"We too had such. In great hours of need, they nursed ill and wounded soldiers. Many a fallen man took comfort dying in the arms of one of those." She sighed and set her sight far off again. "I could not abide such a life. Nor could I marry a man I did not love, have child after child until my body gave out. Nor could I bear to toil in rocky fields and listen to tales of our people being robbed, raped, and killed by brigands. I was trained. I was ready to help!" She pounded one fist against a metal thigh. "I ran away one night. Made my way to the castle and from there established myself as Lord Griffin's best knight.

I did not mingle with the others and after a few scrapes with my blade, the castle and the kingdom left me alone. I earned respect, fighting fiercely by my lord's side. I saved his life more than once. Like you, I have scars to prove my mettle. Early on, I found a youth who pledged his loyalty to me. He knew my secret but was wise for one so young. His eyes, ears and knowledge served me well. No one knew. No one guessed."

She hung her head and sighed, lifting a gloved hand to wipe her cheek. With no secret to keep now, she removed both gloves, laying them on the rock by her hip. With fingers freed of metal, she stretched them several times then dropped them to her lap. "I served many years. Happy years. Yes, I was alone," she nodded to Jake, his question unasked but hanging between them. "But I was at peace with myself. Always in the front of my mind though," she tapped her forehead, "was the knowledge that I might be discovered. The punishment for what I was doing would be quick and brutal. Still, I risked it all. Foolishly. Until the night I discovered my steward, young Felix, dead in our quarters, stabbed so many times his chest was like a leaky boat that would hold no water. I knew who killed the boy. The youthling told me that morn before I rode out with Lord Griffin that Sir Belver had been hounding him, asking why I never stayed with the men. Why this? Why that? Felix was clever but must have slipped up. Belver knew. He wanted me to suffer before he came for me."

"The boy served me faithfully for years. He was a good lad and should have had an honorable death. Knowing my death would soon follow his, I went after Belver. But he'd set a trap and caught me where my lord and himself waited with three castle guards. With them was a man I had heard of but never seen. A man who called himself a mage." She cut her eyes at Jake. "This word means nothing to you?"

"Never heard of such," Jake shook his head, not sure he believed her story. A woman who fought like a man and got away with it? No one suspected all those years?

"Mage is an old word. My father's mother would have used it as a child. But few were alive in my time who called themselves such. This man did. He stood aside while the others destroyed my world. I challenged Belver. And killed him. I had no intention of killing or even injuring my liege, but he looked upon me as if I were an abomination. Unclean. Unpure. A woman fighting in a man's world. He could not let me live. Could not let others know he had been duped."

She turned back to face Jake, tears hanging on her long lashes. She wasn't a beauty. She was tall and muscled. Her plain face, though, showed emotion. He suspected that was one reason why she'd never removed her helmet, besides the fact she was a woman instead of a man. With such an expressive face, she'd never be able to lie to him and get away with it.

"I deserved to be punished. I'd just killed one of Lord Griffin's valuable knights. I wiped Belver's blood from my blade using the man's cape then sheathed my sword, prepared to die. But the mage stepped forward. He'd made plans and wanted to torture me. My lord must have been in on it though I had no idea such a diabolical scheme could exist.

Into the clearing, the guards dragged my parents. Before I could call out and beg mercy for them, the mage—Sir Everrand—motioned, and both lost their heads in front of me. I went mad...mad with grief at the injustice. Their blood yet flowed when one guard brought my destrier into the glen."

"What's a destrier?"

"A magnificent war horse. Big. Beautiful. Gentle. Clever. A blade plunged into his chest took him down. Everything I valued, loved—parents, youthling, faithful steed—was taken from me. Lord Griffin flinched not at the carnage before us as he delivered his verdict. 'You have no name. You are as nothing to me or these people. You broke the Knights Code. This is unforgivable.'"

"They didn't kill you?"

"Nay. They did worse. I lived as you found me. Still in full armor with my weapons, I was tied up and blindfolded, my helm beside me in a cart where the three guards tossed me." She chuckled, but it was not a sound of merriment. "I did not make it easy for them. I had nothing to gain by cooperating so I fought. Hard.

The cart went on at a fast clip. I heard the guards—two common soldiers and the third a captain—speak. I heard the mage directing them each eve. But I received neither bread nor water. Only once was I allowed to relieve myself, and it was ungraceful, humiliating and distasteful.

I determined we stopped on the third day. The soldiers pulled me out, both cautious because I fought. They were not gentle. They placed me on this rock. The moment they would remove the blindfold I was prepared to fight again, ready for a blade to cut me down. That would be an honorable death even though I lied. I was dishonest. But that is not how the mage wanted to leave me. No sooner did I gain my sight than Everrand waved a hand, and I slowed as if fighting in fast moving water. I still wore my armor and had all my weapons. 'Don your helmet, vile vermin' he commanded. I followed his direction though I wanted to fight. I sat as you found me, watching as he waved a hand once more. The three men with him began choking, their bodies turning to ash. With their last breaths, their ashes blew away in the breeze he conjured.

Just we two, he stood before me, his cape black with gold trim heavy enough that winds did not stir it. He smiled at me, but it was as if he wore a death's head mask.

'You will pay for your transgression, woman,' he said as he tried to stare me down. 'But you will not die. You shall remain here forever, aware but unmoving. Always awake. Never sleeping. Always alone. But then you have no idea where you are,' he said as he lifted his hands and gestured to this strange forest. 'Forever alone. Oh, but let's give you hope. Nothing is worse than being alone with hope when no one will ever come.'"

"The mage laughed, and the sound chilled me. 'Let human blood and a single tear spill on your armor, and you shall awaken.' He chuckled as he cut the horse loose from the cart and mounted. 'No one will find you. No one cares,' he said then turned the horse and galloped away." One hand hit her leg in anger. "Damnation, even the mage may be dead by now."

She turned to Jake, one hand out toward him. "Do you understand *alone?* Do you understand *hope*, knowing in your soul that hope is a child's dream?"

"I know loneliness, yes. In the middle of my men, I sometimes feel like I'm on one of those islands I've heard about. A spit of land with water all around. No one else around." He let his gaze fall on the staff across his legs. "I've hoped—prayed—many a time that I live another hour much less another full day. So far—thanks to you—I'm still here, hoping we can get back to where we belong."

"I shall never be back where I belong, as you say, Warrior, for the mage sat me on this rock in the year of our Lord 1025. Over eight hundred years ago. Everything I knew, cared for, loved has long turned to dust."

She finished her tale, gathered her gloves and pulled her sword, in one graceful movement that startled Jake enough that he pushed back on the rock.

Had she lost her mind? In the blink of an eye, she could kill him and leave him dead under the tree where he died once before. Jake's heart pounded, and his mouth went dry. He was trapped between this knight and the tree. Woman or not, she was deadly.

She immediately turned the sword tip down until it touched the ground, the hilt firm in both hands. "What say you, Jacob Border? Can you forgive the lies and the fact I am a woman and not the man you thought I was? Will we journey together, or does your honor demand we travel different paths?" To Jake's horror, she sank to her knees and bowed her head, her forehead resting against the sword hilt. "I will abide by your decision, Warrior."

If her drawing that sword and kneeling scared Jake, waiting for his decision terrified him. He'd never been in a position to decide a person's fate. Well, he rubbed his chin, he had. Every time he guided men into battle. Every time he pulled a trigger, he decided if that person would live or die.

But this...to decide this woman's fate on his word alone. This was too personal. The more he thought about his choice, the more his head hurt. This time his pain wasn't from the wound. His...heart...hurt as well. Lies. She'd lied to her people. Yes, but she was punished in a never-ending way rather than a clean death. She lied to him. She saved his life. She could have removed that helmet while he healed. Then again, she couldn't remove the armor by herself. She was as limited in what she could do as he was when he was so ill.

Anger warred with frustration. "Why did you put me in this position?" he mumbled, his gaze on the top of her head, her dark rich brown hair tied at her neck. She remained silent. Still. Head bowed.

Jake was one who talked out his problems. Usually, he tossed solutions around with his captain. The man was strict but fair with his men. Together Jake and Captain Richmond would come up with a workable fix. But here he didn't have anyone to talk to. Other than the lady knight before him.

Frustration bordering on anger, Jake pushed off his rock and began pacing. He paced around the knight, *hoping*—there was that word she used—hoping for an answer.

"You lied. Spent your life lying. You did good for the people. You lied to me. You saved my life. You could have taken off that damn helmet. Then again, I might not have been so willing to do what you told me to do." He paused then went on. "You know, like resting, eating or walking when I hurt." His hands gestured this way and that. Jake tended to do that when thinking.

"Goddamn you're some kind of lady. A fancy knight..." He searched for what he'd called her earlier. "You're a lady knight. You can out fight me any day of the week." He made a circuit behind her, back and forth. She'd yet to move.

"You were wronged back then by the guy in charge. By that magic man. They had no need to kill all that you loved. A clean death," he studied her. "That's what you wanted. Expected. You knew the risks and figured the good you'd do would outweigh the fact you're a woman. Ain't no woman I know of or ever heard of would—could—do what you did." He paced more then returned to the rock to face her.

He sat thinking about what he would say to the woman. Keeping his deep voice low, he watched her as he got things straight in his head. "Though you didn't die, you paid with your life. I died. You pulled me back. Maybe broke the curse that mage put on you. If we travel together, I need a promise. No more lies, even ones meant to be kind. We don't know where we are. We sure as hell ain't in your time...I don't think. We're not strong if we part ways. We can watch each other's backs until we find other people. When we do..." He scratched his head, wondering what lay ahead. "We'll decide where to go next when that time comes. Sooo..." He took a deep breath, praying this decision would work for both of them.

He stood, took a step closer to the knight, and added one more thing before he gave her his decision. "Lady knight, we travel together. No lies—even kind ones—between us. We protect each other. And I will not take one step further until you tell me your name. The name they took from you. You saved me so I figure I can help you get the name back. It's only right."

Taking a wide stance just in case this woman didn't like what he proposed, he gave her his decision. "Rise, lady knight, and give me your word on these, and we'll decide what happens next." He held the staff ready at his side, hooked one thumb into the edge of his pocket and hoped his world wouldn't fall apart before his eyes.

As if a statue slowly came alive, the woman lifted her head and stared at Jake, perhaps judging his sincerity. Her gaze searched his soul, it seemed. After a full minute, she stood, bent her head to him then lifted it.

"I am unworthy of your words, but I will abide by them." She raised her sword and held it up before her. "I give you no more lies even if doing so hurts. I shall protect you as you will protect me. My parents named me Beatrice. I served my liege lord as Sir William to honor my father who was named such. I will follow your lead, Warrior."

Jake held up a hand right quick. "No, you won't." When the woman opened her mouth to protest, Jake set her straight. "Ain't nobody leading. We go together. We do what we can together. Sometimes I might lead, and sometimes you might. But this ain't all on my back, see."

Beatrice slid her sword into its scabbard and propped her hands on her hips. "Then I request a boon before we venture on."

"What's a *boon*?"

"A great favor."

Jake cut his eyes at her, wondering what might be so important that it would delay leaving. "Ooo-kaay," he said slowly, suspiciously. He wasn't used to this new person, had no idea what she might want. "What's this big favor?" Once more, he hooked a thumb into his pocket.

"A bath in cold clear water."

"Is that all?" Relief hit Jake hard, relaxed him to the point he chuckled.

"And how did your bath make you feel, sir?" Beatrice cocked her head and raised a brow even as a faint smile touched her lips.

"Yeah, okay, I get the point. Not like we have to be somewhere on time or anything." His stomach growled loud enough that Beatrice heard.

"Mayhaps when I smell less like a pig sty, we can venture on and slay a rabbit for our next meal in a new place?"

"Sounds like a plan, lady. Uh, I'll just wait here." He pointed to the rock he'd sat on earlier.

"If you recall, I cannot undo these straps and buckles alone. Many are at my back. If you will stand guard then I may enjoy a hasty bath. Once out, you must help me secure my armor. It is not safe, not wise, to move on without it."

A hint of embarrassment's heat touched Jake. He scrunched up his mouth and pulled a frown so deep his eyes almost disappeared. He turned away from Beatrice, gesturing back toward camp and the stream. "Come on. The sooner this is over, the better." He would have sworn the woman behind him laughed softly. But she followed his longer stride eagerly.

With her back to him, she directed his hands to the buckles and straps that fastened the armor around her. She stood patiently as Jake cussed now and then.

"How the hell do you move with all this on?" He was on one knee undoing the buckles along the back of her thighs. Ready to burst into flames he was so embarrassed, he growled as he spoke, his deep voice making everything he said sound like a threat.

"'Tis the nature of the beast. This armor has served me well. Kept me alive. I would serve it better if I could clean it, but I only have a small linen towel and chemise in my satchel. Nothing to help me care for the steel." She twisted enough to ask, "Are all undone?"

"Yeah, you're ready." Jake quickly turned his back on her but saw her arm as she laid each section of armor in the inverted shield that she'd placed beside him. Her satchel lay at the water's edge. Finally, he saw a pair of leggings and a padded jacket top the pile. Last came a long shirt-type of garment. A moment of silence passed, and then he heard water splash as she stepped in.

"This water is indeed cold. It takes my breath," she spoke. "In truth I will not tarry, or I may die of chills." Water splashed again. "You were a brave man to endure this after your illness," she added. "I will wash my hair then end this madness," she laughed.

Jake wasn't sure exactly what she was doing, but his imagination conjured pictures each time water splashed, and she spoke. Maybe it wasn't a bad idea after all, letting him think her a man while he healed. She was smart enough to know she'd have to confess sooner or later. But knowing *while* he healed could have caused some trouble. Not that Jake would ever take advantage of an unwilling woman but...

Beatrice interrupted him. "Will you move forward several steps? I must dry as best I can then don those disgusting garments again. My cape served you well after you bathed. But this padded coat will not dry any time soon and I cannot travel wrapped only in my cape."

More than willing to put distance between them, Jake moved away from the stream but maintained his vigilance, despite the images she conjured in his mind. They might be interesting but him barely recovered and her not yet dressed left them vulnerable.

"Would you help buckle the cruise and greave on each leg?" Dressed in that long shirt, the padded jacket and leggings, she moved to his side, two pieces in her hand. As Jake buckled and fastened, she named each piece. The fauld of four lames fit round her waist. She held it in place while Jake fixed the straps at her back. "The tassets attach here." She indicated metal shields that hung from the faulds by buckles and protected her upper legs. I can do those," she said and bent to do so as Jake was finishing the buckles at her back.

"Hey, give me a minute to get this one done up." He finished then let her know as he wiped sweat off his forehead and ran a hand over his mustache.

"I beg pardon. I am eager to finish, that's all," she apologized as she lifted two large pieces. She handed one to Jake as she fit the other over her breast. "These pieces are the breastplate. They strap together at the shoulders and sides." That done, she gave him another piece. "The placard also has a front and back. It protects my guts and ribs." Piece by piece, they added steel parts—arm covers and those that covered the shoulders and elbows.

"This takes too long," Jake fussed as he passed her two poleyns or knee covers. "We could be dead and stinking by the time you got all this on."

"Aye. That's why my youthling Felix dressed me each morn and unfastened all each eve. I lived this way all day," Beatrice said as she bent to gather her weapons. "Take this, Warrior." She passed him a knife in a leather scabbard. "I have my boot knife, one here at my side, my blade and shield. I am prepared. You have the knife I gave you before, this smaller one and your staff. You also are as ready as possible." She stood before him, helmet tucked under her left arm, satchel slung over her shoulder and shield now strapped to her back.

If one woman could be the image of both power and gentleness, Beatrice was such a woman. Her clean face glowed with health despite the centuries she'd sat on that rock. Her eyes danced, and she vibrated with what he imagined was a desire to see the world she now occupied. She'd pulled her wet hair back and fastened it at the nape of her neck, out of the way in case she had to put on her helmet in a hurry.

"Looking at you, I feel under dressed," he muttered.

She gave him a small smile as she passed him. "A person trained and ready to defend often needs only heart as his armor. Let us leave this place and find food further along."

"Food, yeah. Good idea." Jake ignored her words about a heart protecting like armor. Silly woman's words, he reasoned. But seeing her move ahead of him, her hand ready to draw the sword, he shook his head and followed. This was no silly woman. This was an interesting but deadly woman, and he needed to remember that.

"You sing. It is a comfort." Beatrice passed the last rabbit leg to Jake. She gnawed the few bits of meat left on her bone then tossed it into the fire.

"Sing? What the heck are you talking about?" Jake finished his meal and tossed his bone into the flames. He had no memory of song or music though he enjoyed both.

"Perhaps *sing* isn't what you would call it? No words, simply a...tune?"

"Humming, you mean?"

"I know not this word, but if music without words is humming then yes, you do this. You do not know you do it perhaps? You have hummed before, as you sat at the fire, watching flames dance as you healed."

"Nah, you're wrong," Jake insisted. He pulled his jacket closer over his chest.

"You are chilled?"

"A little," he admitted. "I wish I had the great coat that the army issued in winter. It was longer. Heavier. With a collar that stood up." He demonstrated turning up the collar on his jacket. "It's cooler here under these trees."

"This armor keeps me warmer than you are. If I offer my cape again, will I offend you?" She made no move to pass it over, waiting for his reaction. "I am close enough to the fire that I will not suffer."

"I'm not suffering. I'm just uncomfortable." He ducked his head and admitted, "I don't sleep so well when it's cold. Reminds me of when I was a kid. Things I'd like to forget." He tossed another limb on the fire. "Besides, we should take turns on guard. Anything around us back where we came from never bothered us, but we're in new territory now. Best to set up a watch." He motioned toward the cape and offered, "Use the cape. Stay warm. I'll take the first watch. We'll switch after a few hours."

"You will wake me? You will not stay awake all night?" Beatrice pulled the long cape to her and stretched out facing the fire.

Jake ignored her. She'd walked all day in boots covered by metal. He figured if she'd once ridden a warhorse every day and then sat like a statue for all those years, she wasn't used to walking for hours.

"Jake." She sighed when he didn't turn around. "I am a knight. I have stood watch before. Do not think you do me favors by letting me sleep till morn."

She was right, but Jake had this thing about women. They were to be protected. Sheltered. Cared for. But this woman had experienced the same things he had. Fighting and killing. She wasn't like the women he had been with or seen up on the ridges, watching men and animals die in battles as if the scene below them were a play.

He had to remember that Beatrice was like him, a soldier. She accepted her responsibilities. Because she did in her time, he had to accept her as an equal.

"Jake?" Her tone of voice indicated her rising anger.

"Okay. Okay. Get some sleep, and I'll wake you in a few hours." He turned back to face a dark denser than any he had ever seen.

She said nothing but quickly settled with her helmet on the ground by her head and her sword on the edge of the cape, one hand curled around the hilt.

With his staff across his lap, ready to push into any attacker, Jake settled in for a long night, hoping his calculation would allow them to share equal time on watch.

Chapter Six
Challenged

"You notice the light?" Jake walked easily beside Beatrice, both ready in case of trouble.

"The trees are thinning. I have yet to see clear sky, but yes, the day seems brighter."

Two days of walking and the dense forest where they found each other was less so. "I'll be glad to see blue sky," Jake muttered. "I'm tired of seeing nothin' but evening."

Further along, Beatrice, who was several feet ahead of Jake stopped so suddenly that he bumped into her. Aware danger might lie ahead, he shifted the staff forward. "What's wrong?"

His eyes scanned the area ahead and had no need for an explanation. "What the hell?"

The tall forest trees had given way to shorter greener trees. But it was the ground beneath them that stopped the two. Pockets of ground lay between tiny streams, as if the brackish-looking water carved meandering gullies in the carpet of short green grass. More light filtered through the trees.

Jake looked up, wondering if his eyes were injured. Without looking for her, his gaze still up at the light, he reached out and swatted Beatrice's arm. "Take a look at this, and tell me if I'm crazy or not."

She stood at his side, close enough that her armor touched his jacket. First, she looked at him, but seeing his gaze focused up, she too studied the sky. "I see no blue. Nor clouds," she said in wonder.

"Nothin' but gold. You ever see anything like that?" He cut his eyes her way long enough to see her shake her head. "First this ground with its islands and now a golden sky. It's pretty," he admitted, "but it ain't natural." He turned a worried face to his companion. "What do you think?"

"This is no land like I have ever seen. And my sky was never this color even in the softest dawn or brightest twilight." She wore an expression that matched his. Eyes darted back and forth, looking for trouble. Tense. Perhaps unnerved.

One hand worried Jake's mustache as he moved his fingers back and forth in thought. "Could be we move a bit more carefully. I hope there's food here and this water is good. But I got a feeling we need to keep our eyes open."

"As if we have not been in that position since the day we met," Beatrice said quietly as she withdrew her sword. "Let us taste the water." She moved to the top of one plot of greenery and went down on one knee.

"Wait!"

Startled, Beatrice stood with sword arm ready. "Where lies the danger, Warrior?"

Jake had the grace to blush. "Nothin' I see but we test the water together. Like you promised—together." He wasn't about to tell her he feared being alone if the water killed her. Better to drink at the same time. If fate took one, it would take both.

Beatrice relaxed her position but didn't sheath her sword. She studied his face long enough to make him fidget.

"We doin' this or not?" he finally said, breaking the awkward silence. He knelt down but waited for her to join him.

She knelt next to him and gave him a soft smile. "I will admit this is a good plan. Going on alone if the water is bad does not please me. As we promised...together." She removed her glove, nodded to him and reached for the water.

Eyes locked on each other, they raised cupped hands and touched lips to the brownish liquid. One sip and they let the rest fall. Then they waited.

Finally, Jake motioned to the water. "We ain't dead yet. Might as well drink our fill. I wish I had a canteen so we could carry some with us." With a nod to Beatrice, he drank several handfuls. She joined him and, with her back to him, ran a wet hand over her face and neck, being careful not to get water on her armor.

"That is not as tasteful at our other stream, but it satisfies my thirst. Let us hope we suffer not for this." Beatrice stood, put on her glove and offered Jake a hand up without looking at him. He accepted, and side by side, they studied the landscape ahead.

"We must eat soon. The rabbit we brought with us is now gone," Beatrice said as she pointed out a path with bigger islands, none larger than what two people could stand on without getting wet.

"Those rabbits like staying around the base of trees. I don't like being too far apart, but maybe if we each move in that direction but along a different path on these islands we can scare up one or two," Jake suggested as he pointed in one direction then the other. Parallel but about twenty feet apart.

"I pray this works. My gut rumbles." Beatrice set off for the right hand path.

"Let's hope that's just hunger and not that water

working on us. Could get messy," Jake said as he took the left path. To his right, he heard Beatrice laugh. A real laugh.

"Would indeed be a mess, as you said, but how you said it was worthy of a court jester."

"Don't know what a jester is," Jake said as he moved forward quietly, hoping to sneak up on a rabbit.

"You have not a person whose purpose is to amuse the court? The people?"

"A comedian? Yeah, we have 'em. I've seen a few in bars. They're paid to keep the customers happy so they'll buy more drinks."

"Just so. Happy drunkards," Beatrice said as she paused, tossed her knife and grinned at Jake across the watery landscape. "I have our next meal. Perhaps you can best that and have something to break our fast on the morrow," she challenged as she lifted a brown rabbit by its odd-looking ears.

"I'll see that bet and raise you," Jake said. He saw her confusion. She didn't understand his poker reference. "Let's see who can bag the most."

Her face lit up as she wiped blood off her knife against the animal's fur. "Challenge accepted."

Later they ate well, eating all of one rabbit and part of another. Three more roasted over the fire. Beatrice glowed over her win. "Tree leaves should keep these clean as we walk," she said as she pulled a pile of large leaves to her side.

"If they don't kill us," Jake commented, grumbling. He'd bagged two to her three. He held up a hand when she shot him a frown. "Yeah, yeah, just kidding." Not sure she understood the term, he added, "I'm being a jester."

That caught Beatrice off guard. She cut a fast glance at him, her mouth hanging open. Then to Jake's surprise, she laughed. A rich hearty sound that went on and on.

Eventually the sound died down as she held her side. "Oh Warrior, I have not enjoyed a jest like that in so long."

She gave him a serious level stare then added, "And you the jester!" That set her off again, her hand on the ground to keep from doubling over in merriment.

"Very funny," Jake sniffed, seeing no humor in what he said. He couldn't deny though that the plain woman had a nice laugh that lit up her eyes and put a pretty smile on her face. But he wasn't telling her that nor was he going to look at her. She read his face and his thoughts too easily.

"Just for that, you can stand first watch." He pulled her cape over, wrapped it around him and laid his staff and one knife at his side, close in case he needed them. Not being so young any more, he was frankly worn out, walking all day though they never moved forward fast. A few deep breaths and he slept.

A sleep that wasn't near long enough. Beatrice knelt next to him, shaking him awake. "Warrior, something comes. Make ready while I cover the fire," she whispered. He rolled out of the cape, held the staff in his right hand and the longer boot knife in the other. Beatrice wore her helmet, her sword in her right hand, her shield on her left arm. "Listen," she said as she moved to his side. "That is no sound I have ever heard. You?"

In the darkness, Jake closed his eyes and listened as the sound drew closer. Not on the ground? Something in the air perhaps? Making a sort of whomp-whomp sound. "Could be something saw the fire. Or smelled those rabbits." Whatever it was was very close. "Behind this tree," he whispered and nudged her sideways. None of these trees was thick enough to hide them, but they were the only defense the two had.

A wider lane through the trees, across the islands, was their path for the next day. But coming up that wide aisle toward them were moving lights. Lights that glowed in the sky, maybe twenty feet off the ground. Lights that moved up and down.

"What the hell is that?" Jake's eyes popped open wide as he made out what kind of thing—creature—was making its way right for them.

"A buterfleoge" Beatrice almost stepped out from behind the tree to get a better look.

"What the hell! Get back here!" Jake jerked her back against him but peered, like she did, at the monster coming toward them. "A butterfly? They don't get that big!" He wasn't sure if he and Beatrice were sharing some strange side effect from the water or not, but one thing he did know: no way could they avoid tangling with the creature.

If seeing a butterfly bigger than a house coming at you wasn't terrifying enough, this one let out a roar like a lion. Not only were the wings lit with strips of bright colors, so was the mouth. One roar with a mouthful of sharp teeth and Jake felt sick.

Beatrice might have as well, but when the thing swooped down toward them, they saw not only the huge wings and nasty looking mouth but feelers that must have been fifteen feet long. Those narrow pieces reached out for them as it made its first pass. Both edged around the tree so the feelers failed to grab either.

"No way out of this. The creature must die," Beatrice yelled as she stepped away from the tree to face the monster's second pass. "Go around the tree, and stab its underbelly while I try to remove those long feelers," she shouted.

They'd never discussed battle plans. Beatrice had fought as many hand-to-hand encounters as Jake probably had. The plan made sense so he edged around the tree as she swung at the butterfly, managing to slice off a small part of a wing. Jake waited until the belly was below him then thrust his staff up with all his might. But the creature was just that much over Jake's head that the staff struck but not deeply enough to do serious injury.

The staff pulled loose as the creature flew past. "We'll get him on the next round," he yelled at Beatrice at the same instance one feeler wrapped around the knight's middle, lifting her in the air. "Bea! No!"

"Jake!" Despite the plea in her voice, Beatrice had her knife out, struggling to hack into the monster's narrow leg. The butterfly slowed as she freed her sword arm, but she had no room to maneuver. "Jake, catch my sword. It's longer. Again but use the sword." The monster was squeezing her. She barely had breath enough to speak.

The sword fell but landed ten feet from Jake. As he scrambled to get it, Beatrice continued to stab the body, bringing it lower. But she was weaker now.

The monster tried to lift with the struggling knight and managed a few extra feet. "The wing. The wing," Beatrice called.

Afraid the monster would fly too high for him to reach then carry off Beatrice, Jake grabbed the heavy sword with both hands. Giving a deep-throated roar of his own, he raised the blade, ran straight to the flyer and only stopped when the edge sheared halfway through the wing.

Injured too badly to fly, the gigantic butterfly flopped onto the ground, its wing useless, but its mouth opened wide. The feeler moved Beatrice toward that fearful maw. Jake ran but slipped. "Bea, the blade!" With all his strength, he sent the sword through the night straight to her hand.

One mighty slash and she sheared away one side of the mouth. As Jake thrust the staff into the heart area, Beatrice sunk her blade into the head through that ravaged mouth.

As the monster collapsed, Beatrice's armor clanked where it rubbed along two-foot-long jagged teeth. She hit the ground hard, her breath knocked out.

The once brightly lit wing fell like a canopy and trapped Jake beneath its weight. He could move but make no headway out.

"Jake! Jake? Where are you?" Beatrice couldn't talk loudly. She still panted from the fight and fall. She rolled over and yelled again.

"Bea? You okay?" Jake's voice came low, shaky as if from far away.

"I survived. But where are you?"

"I think that wing fell on top of me. Stinks in here, and air's getting kind of thin."

Jake heard nothing for a few minutes during which he realized the wing lay sealed against the ground, cutting off his air.

"Talk to me, Jake. I must hack my way to you. The wing is like thick leather. I fear I might hurt you."

"Hurry up. I'm running out of air. Hurry, Bea."

Sounds like an ax against wood reached Jake. He wasn't a church sort of man, but right this minute he prayed Beatrice got to him fast before... The *before* didn't bear thinking about.

One slash landed close enough that it let in cool air. "Careful. You almost got me on that one," he warned her as he lay on his side sucking in air, sour as it was, surrounded by a butterfly carcass.

"Jake? Jake? Where..." Hands moved aside parts of the wing, and Beatrice fell on her knees at his back. "Jake, are you hurt?" Her hands ran down his side and face. He turned toward her, his back lying partly across her lap, his eyes closed.

"I'm too damn old for this shit," he grumbled. "I'm worn out, but I don't think I'm hurt anywhere." His eyes still closed, his breathing better, he let his racing heart calm. "You hurt? Damn thing tried to eat you!"

"I fell from its grasp and landed hard. I lost my breath. Like you, I think fighting a buterfleoge this size is more than I can manage. Together we took it down. Maybe you could have done so alone, but I admit I would have failed."

"We didn't fail, and we aren't in great shape, but best we get out of here before something worse shows up. Blood attracts blood. We made enough noise to wake an army." Heaving a sigh, he rolled off her lap and motioned her to lead the way.

Chapter Seven
Beyond Understanding

Noises sounded louder as the island forest thinned. Neither spoke as they moved forward quietly. Beatrice led the way, her sword and shield held at the ready. Jake walked backwards behind her, guarding their back trail.

Again, Beatrice stopped so suddenly that his back bumped into hers. He took a step up to her side, still searching the area behind them. Though she said nothing, she got his attention when she sheathed the blade, slipped the shield off her arm to let it rest against her leg then removed her helmet—graceful moves that took seconds.

"What is it?" He saw nothing. Heard nothing but the same twitters and scrabbling noises he'd heard for some time now. He took one step further back so he could see her face.

Tears? What the hell?

"Warrior...look." She stood so still he feared more danger, but her face didn't show fear.

Slowly he turned and studied the land before them. Grasslands. Mountains in the distance. He raised his eyes from those distant peaks and gasped. "But...but...that's not possible." He sank to his knees, a hand on the staff all that kept him upright.

Across the grasslands, above the dark outline of rugged peaks hung three moons. One hung over the mountain range, huge, almost as wide as the range. Another moon, much smaller, shone to the right of the monster-sized orb. The third moon—half the size of the largest, hung further back, not quite as bright as its smaller neighbor.

"This is not possible," Beatrice repeated. "My world has one moon, not...not this collection." She stammered as she spoke, her words coming slowly and faint. "Jake, what kind of world did you waken me to?"

He couldn't answer, his focus still on those moons, thinking his brush with death had unsettled his brain.

Beatrice grabbed his shoulder and shook it. When he didn't speak, she dropped her helmet, went down on her knees in front of him and grabbed both shoulders. It's hard to move a bigger person, but she shook him like a dog. "Jacob Border, tell me what in God's name I see! What world is this you live in that has three moons in the night sky?" She screamed at him, tears flowing down cheeks gone so pale, she looked ready to faint. Jake kept staring at the moons, ignoring her. She shook him again. Out of patience, she reared back a hand and slapped him as hard as she could.

That got an immediate response. Jake reached for her throat and pushed her over on to her back. Terror ruled him.

"Jake! Jake!" She fought him, but fear held a firm grip on his mind. Her words came quieter as he choked the life out of her. "Warrior, look...at...m..."

She slumped, no fight left in her, little life left in her.

His hands around a soft warm neck—Beatrice's neck—didn't clear the red from Jake's mind. It was the word *Warrior*. She'd called him that for many days. She believed he was one of those men who is good and fights for justice.

Immediately Jake pulled his hands away, appalled that he'd tried to harm her. He sat straddled on her body, her face red, turned to one side as if he'd broken her neck. Gasping in horror, he bent down to listen for a breath. Feeling one against his cheek, he threw himself off her and started undoing straps and buckles until he could remove the placard across her stomach and the breastplate.

"Come on, damn it, woman. Breathe!" He pulled her into his arms and watched her chest intensely, looking for the rise and fall of the jacket. It was there but so shallow he feared she might not wake. By now, her neck bore bruises shaped like his hands. "Damn! Damn!" He rocked back and forth, berating his temper, praying she would wake so he could beg her forgiveness.

Though she was still unconscious, she shivered. Right there between forest and grass, he tucked her tightly in her cape and held her close, offering his body heat to keep her alive. He could not afford to build a fire in this spot as open as it was. More importantly, he couldn't let her grow cold. So he sat through the rest of the night, watching the three moons sink behind the mountain range, and golden light fill the sky, a light like he'd never seen before.

Dawn broke, and Beatrice coughed. She lay in his arms, covered head to toe in her cape. Only her face was free of cover. She blinked against the light but managed to open her eyes finally. For a long minute, she studied the man whose face she saw.

"Did I die? Did I see what I saw, or was it a dream? A nightmare?" she whispered, wincing because the words hurt her throat. "You tried to kill me?" she asked, amazement in her voice. Anger touched her words as well.

To his shame, Jake hung his head then let his gaze lift to the mountains, still in silhouette, daylight bright behind them. "Yes," he answered honestly.

"Why?" She lay still, either unwilling or unable to move, in shock. "I saved your life," she said vehemently.

"I was scared." Nothing in his life had ever affected him like those moons. He figured there was no word to describe how he felt when he saw them.

Beatrice moved a hand from the cape enough to lay it against his jacket. "You are a warrior...but you are also human, Jake. What scared you so badly that you do this to me?" She gathered his shirt in her hand and shook it, drawing his eyes to her face. "Tell me!" she demanded. "Tell me!"

"That," Jake nodded toward the mountains. "The moons...those three moons." He took a deep breath and hugged her close then loosened her so he could whisper, "How can we be safe? This isn't my world, Bea. I don't know where we are, but this isn't your home...or mine."

Beatrice sat wrapped in her cape. Jake knelt on a knee at her side, close enough that he could catch her if she toppled.

"I do not understand." Beatrice's hand flapped a corner of the material. "Why?"

"Why are we here?" Jake said softly, his gaze going side-to-side, wary of anything jumping them.

"Why you tried to kill me?" The woman slapped Jake's leg hard enough to push him over.

He might have objected at one time, but like soldiers after a major battle or injury, Beatrice was in shock. And it was his fault. He pulled himself up to kneel beside her again, his staff at the ready.

"Tell me, Warrior. Would my death make you feel better, trapped as you are in this strange world with a woman who threatened to kill you?" She spat out the words, refusing to look at him.

"Feel better! If I had choked you to death? With my bare

hands?" He ran fingers through his tangled hair. "Damn it, woman, have you seen those moons? Do you have any idea how we can get home when we don't even know where home is? Damn sure I ain't got none. I was scared shitless. I've never been so scared in my life. I admit it!" He jabbed the blunt end of the staff against the ground. "All my life I've known what to do. But not now," he yelled. "And I'm still scared. Afraid of this," he flung out his hand toward the grasses and mountains, "and scared I might do something like that," he nodded toward her, "again."

"How do I keep us alive? Safe?" He ranted. "It takes both of us to survive, it looks like, after that damn butterfly thing. And seeing the moons...I went crazy. In your world, that may never have happened to you. Damn sure ain't never happened to me. Until that moment. I know you can't forgive me. And I destroyed the trust between us. I regret that the most," he spoke more calmly. "God knows I never meant to hurt you." He turned his face away from her so she'd not see the tears that threatened to slide down his cheeks. With only one person in his entire world, he'd destroyed the thing he valued most: their relationship.

They sat without speaking as the golden light settled into a brassy color that lingered through the day. As the sky settled into its daylight color, Jake finally sat down cross-legged next to her. Neither looked at the other.

He had no idea what Beatrice was thinking. He spent the quiet time remembering his growing-up days when he'd steal food, sleep in abandoned buildings, work long hours for little or no pay and suffer abuse. He'd never trusted anyone. Except one girl. But she was best left in the past.

The army took him in, gave him structure. Taught him how to read, write and do sums. The army gave him a home of sorts with food, clothes and pay. He'd marched, fought, drank and caroused but never met anyone whom he trusted like he did this woman. His sigh came long and sorrowful.

The brassy sky began softening back to gold, the day almost ended. Jake wallowed in regret all day but decided they had to move on. Maybe Beatrice would want to go a separate path despite her pledge to honor his decision to travel together. He couldn't blame her if she did. But he'd miss the company. He wouldn't think past that point.

Tossing aside the grass that he'd woven together, he stood, focused on the dying day beyond the same mountains where the moons would appear. "Guess it's time to move on. I'll gather your gear and see if anything's left of those rabbits." Her hand on his leg stopped him.

"Sit...please," she asked without looking at him.

"You're gonna go your way, and I'm gonna go another," he said and sat with a dejected thump on the grass. "I'll respect your decision. Can't say I'd be surprised. I wouldn't be happy about it. But not surprised. I—"

"Jake, you talk too much."

"Huh?" She'd caught him by surprise.

"We will not always agree. That is human nature. But to exist, we must settle our disagreements and find peace. We are at that point." She pulled the cape tighter around her and rubbed her neck where bruises showed. "I resigned myself to a new world when you told me the year's date. This world was yours. Alone I might have suffered as you did. But I was not alone though you almost died on me several times." She could have smiled at that, but what she said wasn't funny.

"The buterfleoge—the butterfly you called it—scared me but only because you did not recognize it. But together we killed it. Still, I thought of us as in your world. And then we saw that." She nodded to the moons peaking up over the mountaintops. "The way you acted—I knew then this was *not* your world. We were now lost in something—somewhere—some time neither knows. But," she paused with emphasis, "we are together as we pledged. We can face whatever might come. Mayhaps we will live. Mayhaps we will die."

She finally looked at him for the first time in hours. "Do you recall what I said to you when I told you how we met? About dying alone?"

"Something about dying alone ain't so bad but," Jake took a few seconds to remember. "To die so near another and not receive comfort in passing ain't right."

"Well recalled."

Jake started to say something, but she held up a hand. "Let me finish...please. You recall also I spoke of my youthling squire's death?" Jake nodded, and she continued. "I did not tell you the entire story. I must now in order to mend this broken kinship."

"I knew of Belver's questioning. Worried about it all that day. The man was a ruthless tyrant disguised as a knight. Loyal to my liege lord's face but bullying others behind the man's back. And then I found the boy—butchered." Beatrice reached out and pulled some grass. Like Jake, she began weaving the stems together. "Like you, I went mad. With grief. I killed six men in order to get to Belver. No matter that he set a trap, I went after him the instant I saw him. I was not scared of him. I wanted to avenge the boy. I hacked him through armor and exposed body. When the soldiers dragged in my parents and then my horse, I was terrified. It was then I was scared. Like you were. I knew not when the final blow would come. Later I knew not why I still lived. As I sank into that long slumber, I knew fear."

Beatrice threw the grass aside and pulled the cape back around her. "The boy, my parents, that beloved steed, died without comfort. I should have died many times and would have accepted it as my due."

"Like me, this past night, you saw a new world. You feared. You reacted as I did—hitting out at the first thing you could find. Raging at the injustice. The unexplainable," she said and gestured around them. "I cannot condemn you for what you did. For I have done the same and worse. We must be honest with each other and leave the past behind." She again looked him in the face.

"We know not where or when. But we must face tomorrow together because you and me...we're all we have." Jake repeated the words she told him long ago. "Like the pledge, together." He breathed deeply, the first time that day free of worry. "Fresh start tomorrow."

"Indeed, fellow warrior. A new day. Together."

Beatrice once more stood in full body armor, her helmet held under one arm. Together she and Jake studied the landscape. She gestured out over the grassy plain. "This appears to be a valley between two ranges." She pointed to the right. "The moons and daylight come from there." She gestured to the left. "We have seen nothing to remark those peaks."

"In the army, we faced our opponent across wide fields like this. Each side knew the other was there. We also knew what to expect within the area between us. Maybe deer or hogs. But nothing like we ran into with that flying creature." He used one hand to shade his eyes, checking out first one range then the other. "We'd be smart to avoid that tall grass. It's only up to my belt, but lots of dangerous things could hide in there and get us before we know what's happenin'." He lifted a shoulder in a shrug. "Makes no never mind which way we go, I guess. What do you think?"

Beatrice pointed to the range on their right. "We saw

those mountains first. I say we venture there and see where those moons come from."

"My thinkin' too." He curved his hand to indicate a path. "We'll follow the edge of this plain. Stay in the foothills. That'll give us some cover if anythin' comes after us."

"I wager those mountains are not as close as we wish." She sighed as she hefted her shield.

"I bet they're a lot taller than we think."

Three days later, hungry and thirsty, she looked at him. "Further than I thought."

He nodded to her. "And a damn sight taller than I thought."

"Warrior, those are snow-capped peaks. The tree line comes close to the valley floor, and snow hangs from many branches. We have no defense against that kind of cold." Beatrice sat on a rock, her eyes scanning for a path.

Jake stood some distance away, hand on hip, a frown pulling a line between his brows. "I wish I knew if this is summer or winter here. Or the times between them."

"Have we had good fortune so far or is trouble yet to come?" Beatrice commented.

"Don't know but we gotta get something to eat and drink soon, or we're gonna pass out on the trail," he said as he returned to his companion. He pointed further up the mountainside. "See that patch of trees up there?" Beatrice took a few seconds to spot what he was talking about. "Do you see how those flowers trail down to the foothills below?"

"Water, do you think?"

"Possibly. Can't hurt to check it out." He grinned and held out a hand. "Let's get a move on, you lazy knight," he teased. They were worn out, Beatrice especially in her armor, heavy shield and sword.

"Ah, playing the jester again," Beatrice said as she clasped his hand and let him pull her up. "Your humor does not grow with time," she said with one brow lifted. "Lead on, Warrior."

Jake's instincts proved correct. They fell on tired knees and sampled the water, same as they'd done at the island trees—at the same time. Pure tasting, clear and freezing cold, they drank slowly.

Beatrice collapsed onto the ground and hung her head, weariness written on her face. "I could die a happy woman this instance. That water was nectar."

"What's *nectar*?" Jake asked as he drank another handful.

"Nectar? Uh, the finest thing you have ever had to drink."

"I've had nectar then...before this." He'd pulled off his jacket. "Those first sips of water you gave me, remember. Now that was nectar." He pulled his shirt off over his head. He lay on his stomach, splashing water through his hair, up his arms and neck. He got up on a knee and ran wet hands over his stomach, completely forgetting his companion in the joy of being at least cleaner than he had been. Shaking his wet hair, he collapsed, sitting cross-legged. With a sigh, he lay back, closed his eyes.

He may have slept...probably did. Eventually he sat up, stretched and pulled his shirt to him.

He remained seated but swiveled enough to see Beatrice. She sat with one knee bent under and the other propped up. One arm dangled off the knee, and the other rested on the ground. If Jake hadn't known her to be a woman, he'd have sworn his companion was a man. The expression on her face, however, said she was all woman and fuming about something.

"What'd I do now?" He'd been with enough bar maids and women of the night—and maybe a married woman or two—to recognize trouble.

"You bathe when I cannot. Tis too dangerous to remove my armor in this strange land," she fumed. "You show..."

Immediately she snapped her mouth shut, rolled to one side, and stood. In a huff, she stomped off, following the stream they'd found. She left Jake sitting alone with his mouth hanging open.

"What the hell was that all about?" he grumbled as he pulled on his shirt and coat. An over-sized bird fluttered to a branch over his head and began making a racket as if fussing.

"Uh maybe I better just stay here. Guard her things." Beatrice had stomped off, leaving her helmet, sword and shield behind. No matter how angry she might be, she'd return. "Damn women," he told the bird even as he reached for his staff.

By the time she returned, Jake had a small fire going and the bird's carcass roasting. Nearby lay a pile of colorful feathers.

She plopped down beside him and accepted the meat he offered. She passed both wooden cups to him, and he returned with cold water. "'Tis not fair," she finally said after taking a savage bite.

Best to let her get it out, whatever's stuck in her craw, Jake decided. However, whatever she meant to say stayed within her. She seemed calmer. Resigned. Resigned to what he had no idea.

"You still mad at me?" he finally ventured to ask. He wouldn't sleep well if there wasn't peace between them. "You sort of stomped when you left earlier." If he could make her laugh, then balance would be restored. For her, he didn't mind being a jester.

"No," she sighed. "Men cannot help such things, I suppose." Again, she sighed then changed the subject. "Who has first watch?"

"You, I guess. I stayed awake last night making sure you didn't die on me," he said with a small grin. "Who'd protect me if you died?"

"Perhaps not the finest thought, Warrior. You would survive. Sleep well, Jake. I will protect you as I know you will me." With those cryptic words, she gathered her things and took up a position away from the fire, her gaze outward.

"Night, Bea," Jake said quietly as he pulled the cape over him.

Some time later..."Warrior! To me!"

Jake rolled over, grabbed his staff as a man ran toward him. A stranger with a wicked steel-looking pike. A leather-like helmet covered his face. That didn't disguise the bellow the man gave as he aimed to skewer Jake.

He managed to dodge the initial attack only because he was low already. Turning to face another attack, he heard metal clang against metal. That would be Beatrice's sword warding off another man? Dodge, duck, defend. Behind him, he heard her issue a battle cry. Was she driving back her attacker?

With no idea how many foe they faced, Jake pulled up battle energy of his own and grabbed the pike the next time the man came for him. With all hands engaged, face to face, Jake took aim at the man's knee and kicked as hard as possible. Bone crunched loud enough to hear. The man went down with a scream. He turned to help Bea, but a pike to the side of the head took him out.

Chapter Eight
Stunning but Strange

His head hurt badly. His eyes squeezed shut, his head pounding, he could barely breathe for the pain. His mind drifted. He saw a knight. Then a woman. Darkness. A giant butterfly. Gentle hands on his body. Fever. Cold. A nightmare? A dream?

No, those were memories. As the immediate pain lessened, Jake remembered. Beatrice. Where was she?

"Bea?" Hearing no response, he called again. He lay in darkness on something soft but firm. "Bea?" Worry grew to fear. Perhaps she couldn't hear him. "Beatrice," he yelled as loudly as he could. One hand went to his head where pain flared stronger. "Damn it, where are you?"

He turned but saw little. A faint glow illuminated a small space on the far side of the room, leaving several dark corners. Room? Turning more, he felt coolness along his back. Not unpleasant. At that point, he realized he wore nothing. A sheet of some kind—smooth and silky—covered him. But nothing else.

"Beatrice, where the hell are you!" Desperate now to find her, he sat up and pulled the sheet around his waist. Both feet touched the floor, but his head swam. Unable to remain conscious, he fell back on the bed.

When he opened his eyes next, his first impulse was to yell for Bea again, but the vision before him left him breathless with his mouth hanging open.

Standing next to his bed, bathed in soft light from a nearby lamp, was the most beautiful woman he'd ever seen or even imagined. Midnight black hair fell in waves behind her with strands falling over her shoulders to lay on her... Jake sucked in air so deep he almost gagged. A sheer drape covered her, clasped at the shoulders, with narrow—very narrow—stripes going down to barely cover the fullness of her breasts. A jewel-encrusted belt cinched the drape at her waist, but the material didn't cover her legs, simply went down, leaving her thighs bare. At least as far as he could see, lying on his back, his manhood straining toward her like a magnet to iron. He barely managed to pull his eyes to her face as he moved one hand under the sheet in an effort to push down his shaft.

Fighting himself, he managed to see brilliant blue eyes in a delicate white face, high cheekbones with a faint blush and the most kissable mouth he'd ever seen or dreamed of. A sigh of longing escaped him.

She addressed him. But he didn't recognize a word. His lack of understanding had little to do with the raging hard between his legs.

While his face must have shown what he was thinking—amazing woman, bed her—she watched him with a growing frown. If she was confused, so was he. Was this another part of the world he and Beatrice now lived in?

Like a man coming out of a delicious dream, Jake forgot about hiding his desire, grabbed his sheet and yelled at the top of his voice, "Bea! Where the hell are you?"

To his surprise, she answered in a fuzzy not-yet-awake

voice...from a dark corner behind the ravishing beauty standing before him. "Jake?"

"Here! I'm here, Bea. Are you all right?"

She didn't answer.

"Beatrice, answer me now," he bellowed.

"I'm here, Jake, but I don't know..." Her voice faded.

Trying to see around the sensual creature, Jake craned his neck. "Bea?" Hearing nothing from across the room, he turned imploring eyes on the woman. "Please," he begged, gesturing toward Beatrice.

The woman didn't understand. She left the room as if he hadn't spoken.

Gathering the sheet, his feet on the floor once more, Jake took deep breaths to ward off collapsing again. His head hurt, but then he'd been there before. Using the side of the low narrow bed, he moved to the wall, using it to stay upright until he found her.

Like him, she lay beneath a thin sheet. Used to seeing her in leggings and a padded jacket, he paused a moment, glad she'd survived but curious as to what she really looked like, covered as she always was.

Her brown hair laid spread out around her, a little longer than he thought it might be. Her shoulders, so broad in armor, still appeared so but more feminine. The bruises on her neck hadn't faded much in the days since he tried to choke her to death. That alone shamed him. Her arms lay on top of the sheet, her fingers long and slender out of the leather gloves. With arms at her side, the sheet pulled enough over her body to give him a view of small breasts, narrow hips and a darker area between her legs.

In his distress at trying to find her, his manhood had calmed. But seeing her like this made him see her not as a knight or a companion or fellow soldier. He saw her as a woman.

Despite this moment of clarity, his heart relaxed at knowing she lived. Together they could figure out what was going on. He leaned over, elbows on the bed next to her, his fistful of sheet held at his chest. He searched her face then softly called to her. "Bea?"

She muttered, but he couldn't understand what she said. She fidgeted a little but didn't open her eyes.

"Beatrice? It's me. Wake up." He watched her intently, hoping she wasn't so injured in battle that she had fallen unconscious. "Bea, it's me, Jake. Please wake up," he pleaded. In this new world, in this place at this moment, he needed her strength to balance his fear for her.

"Jake?" she breathed on a long sigh.

"Can you open your eyes for me, Bea?" He moved in closer and lifted her head. "Come on, open your eyes." Thankfully, she did as he asked. Opened pain-filled storm-gray eyes. Seeing him, she tried to lift her hand to touch him. She was too tired. Maybe too weak but she smiled. "Are you well?"

"Yeah, yeah. And you'll be okay too. Just rest." Jake laid her head down and stroked her hair. "Don't you go dying on me now."

"Always the jester," she whispered, closing her eyes but turning her head so it rested against his hand. With a soft sigh, she returned to sleep.

Her bed, like his, was too narrow to share, but he wasn't leaving her. Never alone if he could help it. She sat without anyone for too many centuries to be alone now. He sank to the floor, let his head fall back against her bedding and waited.

The same woman returned later. By her side stood a handsome man. Jake knew this man could break a dozen hearts with his wavy black hair, green eyes and chiseled features.

He also sensed the man could hide traits not so appealing, but then he might be a bit jealous. He'd never seen such a perfectly matched pair. A dazzling couple, her in the sheer outfit and the man in similar material, held together by a broad jeweled belt that rode between waist and hip. Over the sheer fabric lay a curved piece of leather. Over the curved piece lay thin strips of that same leather, each strip heavy with jewels. Other than the thigh-length fabric and belt, the man wore nothing else but thin sandals tied at the ankles.

The man spoke, pointing to Jake then Beatrice. Whatever he said was a question. Jake didn't know the language. He'd never heard such nor seen such perfect looking people.

Not sure what they wanted, he touched his chest. "Jake." He patted his chest and repeated, "I'm Jake." He levered his body up until he could stand beside Bea's bed. He pointed at her, touched her hand and said, "This is Beatrice." Like talking to a child, he touched her shoulder. "Beatrice."

"Jake?" Bea stirred and put a hand to her head. She saw him near her but not the other two. She grabbed his arm, intent on sitting up.

"Uh, Bea, you might want to gather that sheet 'cause you ain't wearing anything," Jake warned her without taking his eyes off the man and woman. Both watched Jake and Bea intently, studying them like specimens.

Beside him, he heard Bea gasp.

"Yeah, nothing there," confirming she was as naked under her sheet as he was under his. She used his arm to sit up then turned so her legs hung off the bed. "Best not try to stand," he warned again. "The first time didn't work so well for me." She finally turned enough so her bare shoulder and arm touched his. For the first time since he'd opened his eyes in this place, he felt balanced.

"Who are they, Jake?"

"No idea. I don't understand what they're saying." He glanced down to reassure Bea but recognized her expression. The same one he had earlier. Her mouth hung open, her eyes were wide, eyes that traveled up then down the man's body. She gasped several times as her eyes moved.

Breaking off, she looked up at Jake, wonder in her gaze. "He is truly beautiful," she whispered in an awe-struck voice. Her tongue caressed her lips, licking them like she might want to lick that man.

That didn't set well with Jake. That man was a distraction. He rolled his eyes at Bea who snapped out of the man's entrancement long enough to blush. A color that didn't stop her nipples from rising to hard points.

Jake couldn't say much. Seeing the beauty with the man then Bea's reaction, his shaft began to fill. To cover that and his coming embarrassment he bunched the sheet fuller in front of his body.

He and Beatrice stared at the couple, unable to communicate. After several awkward minutes and a back and forth conversation between the beautiful couple, the man called to someone in a hall beyond the room. Several women entered the room, listened to his instructions then bowed to the couple as they left.

Beatrice didn't seem affected by the women but one look at Jake told her he was. Once more, he stood like a statute, awed by the incredible beauties in the room. For these four women were as magnificent as the first woman.

Two moved to Jake's side while two stood near Bea. His head swiveled, trying to take them in. They wore a narrow band across their breasts and a thin loincloth at their hips.

To Jake, they were as naked as he'd ever seen a woman. Even the prostitutes he visited wore more clothes when they caroused than these four.

His mouth went dry, his lips parched until his tongue came out. Sweat covered his face while his shaft practically bounced in its need. A very sturdy sharp elbow in his ribs broke the trance.

Beatrice refused to look at him. She allowed two of the beauties to ease her off the bed and support her as they guided her out of the room.

"Hey, wait a minute!" Jake called. "Where she goes, I go," he got out just as the remaining women gestured for him to do just that—follow Bea. He hustled to catch up with her, but the group only went twenty feet further down the same hall to closed doors.

Opening the double doors, they escorted Jake and Bea into a room slightly larger than the one they just left. No windows. A high ceiling and in the middle—water. Steaming water. A bath?

Jake wasn't sure which one of them headed to the water first, but he went to one side while Bea went to the other. Suddenly the two stood facing each other, their sheets loosened, but exposing little more than either had already seen.

"Uh, Bea? What do we do now? I ain't never took a bath with ladies around," he gestured to them, flapping a hand at her.

Bea gave it a minute's thought. "Once in the water, we will not feel so uncomfortable? You turn, and I enter then I will..."

Jake was nodding already as he turned. "Go ahead." The women next to him watched the others. When water splashed softly, Jake still didn't turn.

"I will turn now, Jake. Come in. This is heavenly."

Still Jake didn't move. One woman with him moved

onto steps hidden in the water. Seeing no progress, the woman at his side took him by surprise and forcibly snatch away his sheet, leaving him buck-naked. In a flash, he took the steps into the water, sinking into the warmth up to his neck. All four of the women giggled.

"Are you well, Jake?" Beatrice stood in water to her shoulders, her back to him so she had no idea what the woman did to get him in the water.

"Yeah, but this one's a mean bitch," he grumbled even as he ducked his head under water. "Damn, this feels good."

"Indeed. I am turning around now. I am not fond of speaking to you like this." She turned to discover they stood about five feet apart.

"This spot looked bigger when we walked in," he gestured with a wet hand. "We're here now though. I have no idea what's going to happen next or how long we can stay here, but I'm gonna get really clean." So saying, he looked for a cloth and soap. The woman on his right held up a cloth while the one on the left held a pot of what might be soap.

The two refused to give him either, instead advancing on him after dipping the cloth into the pot. Immediately Jake began backing up, only to remember it was a small pool crowded with Bea and two other women.

"No! Get away!" Jake splashed water at the two advancing on him. "No!" he bellowed again, his heart pounding, embarrassment flooding his body with a hot blush.

Behind him, he heard several women laughing, but they weren't Bea. He'd heard her laugh enough that he'd recognize it. Still his two women attempted to bathe him.

"Bea, help!" This time he heard a soft chuckle. "This ain't funny, woman," he snapped as a hand eased onto one shoulder. He started to push it off, afraid the four would gang up on him.

"Peace," Beatrice said as she held up a hand to stop the women. Without drama, she motioned for all to leave the pool. She indicated they could sit at the edge of the water. She stood at his side with her hand on his shoulder. She gestured for the cloth and motioned them to put the pot on the edge of the pool. When everyone was out but her and Jake, she made her way to the pot, scooped out some white substance and returned to Jake. "All is well now, Warrior," she said with a glance that told him she was laughing at him.

"Humph," he snorted but began scrubbing his face. Behind him, Bea splashed as well. When he rinsed his face, he looked over his shoulder to see what Beatrice was doing, but she wasn't there. In a sudden panic, he pushed his way to where she'd been. In such a small pool, he should have thought of the possibility he might run into her. Sure enough, she came up practically in his arms.

"Bea? You okay?" He grabbed her shoulders to steady her, water running off her hair.

"My hair has not been cleaned far longer than anyone knows," she laughed as she held his arm. "*You* know how long, but oh, this feels so good!"

He splashed a handful of water at her. "I thought you drowned." His grumpiness covered worry.

Taking back her hand and bringing it around to him, pushing a good measure of water, Beatrice managed to hit him full body with water. She laughed at him and fell backwards, sinking below the surface to rise up like a goddess, laughing and dripping wet.

Jake swatted her with water again, and for a few minutes, the two played, having fun. Their time together up to this point only meant survival.

When they separated at last, he edged to the side of the pool, away from the four watching. He'd forgotten about them. Bea continued to use cloth and soap, dipping under water now and then.

She came up sputtering and laughing at the same time. "The water is just deep enough that I cannot stand properly to wash my toes. She leaned over while apparently trying to pull up her foot. Over she went, again coming up spitting out water. "I will try sitting on the step maybe?" Even as she said that the thought must have occurred to both of them that she'd be exposed to his view.

"Give over the foot, helpless knight," Jake said as he gestured her closer. He held out a hand, added soap to the cloth she gave him then waited for her to put her foot in his hand. When he saw her hesitate, he couldn't resist teasing. "Not afraid, are you, Warrior?" He arched a brow at her and waited.

"Helpless?" She snorted as she swam to the ledge next to him. "Afraid? Only if you tangle up my toes," she snapped at him, her nose in the air.

"Give over," Jake repeated then reached down and grabbed one of her legs. Hoisting it caused her head to go under as she grabbed for the pool's edge. He proceeded to wash each toe, careful not to spread them too far apart, as they were small and fragile-looking. One foot finished, he dunked her foot several times to rinse off the bubbling soap. Before he could reach for her leg, she swatted the water to ward off his hand. She hoisted her other foot so high and fast she almost bumped him in the nose. He gave a sour frown that she ignored as he repeated the process.

Once done, Beatrice pushed off from his side and made soft waves in the water.

Cloth in one hand, filled with soap, Jake attacked the last spot that needed cleaning—his back. His hand over his shoulder and a few cuss words didn't quite get the middle of his back washed.

"Need help?" Beatrice played near him, a silly grin on her face as she lifted a handful of water and let it dribble out around her fingers.

"Nope, I'm good," Jake insisted even as he almost pulled a muscle in his side trying to reach a place in the middle of his back that began itching. The itch drove him nuts. He figured it was the Lord getting him back for dunkin' Bea earlier. "You win, damn it. That spot in the middle of my back itches like fury." He tossed the cloth over his shoulder, knowing she'd waited him out and would catch it. She knew him too well.

"Right here?" She held his shoulder as the cloth scrubbed the center of his back.

"Oh yeah, right there," he crooned, his eyes closed, his world perfect. The spot moved, so for a few minutes, Beatrice followed his directions—left, down, a little higher—until he relaxed. As he relaxed, she added soap to the cloth once more and gave his back a hearty scrubbing from shoulders to water line. "Damn, that feels good." He sighed as she brushed thick soap off his back.

"Rinse that off, or you may itch again," she directed.

He ducked and rose only to duck under again, her hand on his shoulder, brushing off his back.

When they finally leaned against the pool's side, Beatrice commented on the water as she chased a stray bubble away. "Per chance this is one of those pools that has water flowing through it to a river? The water is as lovely, clear and warm as when we entered."

Jake shrugged, his eyes closed. "I wish I could just stretch out and float for a while."

"Aye, would be soothing," she agreed, also with eyes closed, head leaning back on a curved edge.

Jake knew why he didn't float. With the women about, he wasn't about to float on his back with his shaft pointing straight up. That happened every time he saw these women. He'd forgotten about them during his bath but thinking about them now—he cracked an eyelid open enough to see two of them in their water-heavy drapes. Drapes that turned invisible when wet. To his dismay, his shaft stood out proudly. How was he going to get out of this pool like that?

He cut a glance to Bea, wondering what she was thinking. He figured she didn't float for the same reason—parts of her would stick out proudly above the water. If she floated at the surface, the lower part of her might also be exposed.

No matter how he'd get past his two women, he wasn't staying this near Bea in this condition. "You think it's time we should get out?" He held up one hand. "My fingers are getting wrinkly."

Bea held up a hand, surprise on her face. "I as well have this skin." She acted as if she'd never seen such.

"You ain't never seen your skin like that after a long time in the water?"

"I have never been in water this long," she admitted, still examining her hand. "I have never enjoyed a bath as much as this one." Aware of what she revealed, she blushed. When Jake grinned, she gave him a frown and swatted water at him. She waded toward the steps leading out the pool.

Immediately the four women hopped up, gathering huge towels.

Jake turned his back on Beatrice as she left the water. His concern now was the two who stood ready with a towel big enough to cover him from wet head to toes. Still stiff, he gritted his teeth, dashed up the steps and grabbed for the towel before they knew what he planned. In the end, he figured he was even with the one who snatched his towel away earlier.

They left wet footprints in the hall as the women directed them back to their room. It wasn't hard to see the quartet intended to dry off their charges. Jake swatted away four hands even as he called for help. "Bea, make them leave me alone."

Once again, she stopped the women and motioned them out of the room. One nodded, spoke to the others and they left. The last one went to a set of doors and opened them to indicate a small and large pull-on long shirt. She laid the small one on Beatrice's bed and the large one on Jake's. Then she opened a door at the end of the room, letting them see it was an indoor privy, what Jake called a bathroom. He'd seen them in finer homes where his officers lived. No need to search for a place to relieve oneself. Giving each a nod, the beautiful woman left them alone.

They stood like mummies, wrapped in their towels. Without purpose for the first time since they met.

Jake began drying his hair, using one end of the sheet. He worked around himself until the last place left lay below his waist. Sitting on the edge of his bed, the sheet laid over his lap, he pulled on the shirt. It wasn't much, a front and back with no sleeves or collar. He also found no drawers. His privates simply hung in air beneath the fabric. "Ain't much to this, is there?" he said as he plucked the shirt at his chest.

"Indeed," Beatrice said. She'd taken advantage of Jake drying off to don her own sack-like shirt. "After wearing armor for so long however, I will say this is freer."

"A little too free, if you ask me."

Beatrice gave him a cheeky grin as if she read his mind.

To distract her, Jake moved to her side of the room, a matter of four steps. "Let me see your neck. I wanna check on those bruises. No telling what these people think of me after seeing them."

"They will not see you as a raw brute, so calm your worries," she said as she let him turn her head one way then another.

"They're not as dark as they were, but I still see fingerprints."

"I am well so do not fret." She took her sheet and his, fluffed them then laid them out on the floor in an empty corner. "Jake, where is my armor? My blade and weapons? Have these people discarded them?" Her eyes watered.

"I reckon it's stored somewhere. I don't think they'd throw away the armor. But I bet someone got a shock when they took off your helmet and found a woman instead of a man," he chuckled, the image in his mind quite funny.

"How do I even ask about it?" She returned to her bed and sat. "What now?"

Jake shrugged. "Now we wait."

Yet another stunning woman came in sometime later. This one wore a few more clothes but not by a long shot, Jake reckoned. A long piece of sheer material wrapped several times around her chest and tied at the waist. A jeweled belt lay over that, holding in a length of fabric down the middle and back of her but leaving her sides exposed. Delicate sandals adorned her slender feet.

She carried a tray heavy with food. Leaving it on a stand at the end of Jake's bed, she turned and left without saying a word.

That same reaction happened again. Jake's shaft strained toward this stranger. "I can't take much more of this," he muttered. A fresh sheet lay on each bed, and he pulled his over his lap.

His problem transferred to Beatrice just then when that same man who visited earlier returned. He nodded to both but spoke to Jake. Though Jake tried to catch anything that might sound familiar, he heard nothing. Beatrice stood behind the man, visibly panting. If she'd been a dog with a large bone, she would have been drooling. Jake didn't dare turn his attention from the man to roll his eyes at Bea, however.

Finally, the man stopped speaking. He placed both hands on exposed hip bones, sighed quite obviously in frustration and turned to leave, putting him face to face with Beatrice. Jake had no idea what the man did, but Bea looked like melting butter. It was disgusting how she acted. He shook his head.

When the man left, she stood, apparently lost in some dream world.

Wadding up a cloth from the dinner tray, Jake tossed it at his companion, hitting her at the temple. She awoke and gave him a bewildered look. "Why did you hit me?" She knew what hit her was soft but had no idea why he did what he did.

"You were drooling. It was disgusting." He tore off a piece of bread and dipped it in what smelled like soup.

"Drool... Me?" Beatrice's mouth hung open, her eyes wide in disbelief.

"Oh yeah. I could almost see your heartbeats from across the room...in near dark."

"I never..."

Calmly eating, Jake shook his finger at her. "You'd have gone with him in a heartbeat if he'd flicked his finger at you." He'd be the last one to admit he might be a bit jealous.

Beatrice copied him with the bread and soup, but she brought the tray with her and placed it on his bed. She sat at one end of it while he sat at the other end. Only the tray's length separated them.

She wasn't above getting her own back, however. Jake should have known better than to open the subject of reactions.

"I do not have to imagine your reaction to the beauteous females who have paraded around you since we arrived." She sipped soup nonchalantly, ignoring his suspicious frown.

"I ain't had no *reaction*," he lied, watching her out of the side of his eye.

She snorted. "We promised no lies—even those that might hurt, Warrior." She used a piece of bread to point directly at his lap. "Me thinks that hurts every time you see one of these females." She wagged her brows at him but kept eating, her legs crossed on his bed, her shirt long enough to cover the upper parts of her legs and that darkness between her legs. "You cannot walk properly at times," she delivered a final thought.

"You can walk, but those points up there and your panting are give-aways."

She frowned but glanced down at her breasts where her nipples raised hard peaks.

"I wonder..." Beatrice began but shook her head as if her thought wasn't worth her effort.

"Wonder what?" Jake finished a cup of wine with the comment, "Good stuff."

"Just an idea that I must study." She dusted bread-crumbs into her hand then wiped them off onto the tray.

"Finished?" She stood, prepared to move the tray back to the stand.

"I can do that," Jake offered.

But she waved him off. "Best I do this. You might be uncomfortable carrying it," she explained then gave a funny choking sound.

"Hey, this isn't funny."

"It is a bit. We both suffer when these creatures come around. Some of us just hide it a bit better." She did laugh then but covered it with her hand. She sat back down on his bed. "We will deal with this as best we can." She snickered and nudged him in the side with that same sharp elbow. "Laugh, Jake, or you will become a grumpy old man."

"Grumpy?" He refused to look at her. "And I ain't old," he added, his nose in the air, figuratively out of joint.

"'Tis whatever you say, Warrior," she whispered as the lights in their room and hall dimmed. "No sun to guide us from dawn to twilight but I think it be time to rest." Touching his arm without a laugh or tease, she eased off his bed. "Sleep well."

He humphed, still a bit put out by her observations. They'd traded barbs, but he didn't want to harm her.

"Bea?" He lay under his sheet, his body finally calmed.

"Aye?"

He heard her rustling, probably getting comfortable. He didn't know exactly what he wanted to say.

"Aye?" she repeated with a yawn.

If he had any chance for a tranquil night's sleep, he had to make peace with her. "I didn't mean to hurt your feelings. I'm not happy about how this whole thing is happening." He fidgeted then turned on his side toward her. "I'm sorry."

She didn't answer right off.

Maybe she'd fallen asleep.

"Jake? I meant no harm. This is strange. But we will be fine...as long as we stay together. Sleep well, Warrior."

His mind as calm as his shaft, he sighed, crossed his hands over his chest and clung to her words.

Chapter Nine
Together but Not

T*ogether* didn't last long. The next morning when the lights grew brighter in their room and the hall, a woman brought another tray. They ate slowly.

"What are we going to do, Jake? We know not our fate. Are these people waiting on something? We understand them not nor they us. 'Tis frustrating and..." She finished a cup of something that was warm and favorable and set it back on the tray that lay on her bed this time. "'Tis frightening as well."

Jake sat on the floor, his cup resting in his lap, his legs crossed at the ankles. He'd dragged his sheet down to cover himself when the woman entered, a fact neither alluded to. "Hey, come over here." He patted the floor next to him. "I don't know what they want." Beatrice settled down, her shoulder near his arm. He fluffed part of his sheet over her legs. "We wait, I guess."

They sat quietly for a long time, each lost in thought.

"My goal was to get back to my unit, my men. Help finish up the war and survive if possible. I met you and the goal sort of stayed the same. I want to return but get you back to my people and keep you safe doing it." He waved his hand as he usually did when speaking and added, "This, though. I don't know what to make of giant butterflies and men and women speaking a language I don't recognize or being so damn beautiful that I ache whenever one of them shows up." He frowned down at the cup. "It's embarrassing and hurtful." He turned his head to show his companion a worried face. "How can I get you home safely when we ain't home, and we aren't safe most of the time?"

"You speak of goals," Beatrice said as she placed a hand on Jake's arm and squeezed it in commiseration. "My goal was to fight for my people. The mage deprived me of that. I found you and realized I didn't want to be alone. The year—I knew I would not return from whence I came, but I would instead follow you to your people. Like you, I cannot plan, cannot create another goal beyond staying alive each day. We are like a ship an old mariner told me of once. Ships need a rudder to keep them going in the right direction. Without that, a ship is at the mercy of wind and wave." She patted Jake's arm, pulled the sheet across her shoulders and moved closer to his side. "I fear we are without a rudder, Warrior."

Without daylight, neither had any idea how long they sat. Another tray came, delivered by a man as handsome as the first with the usual reaction on Beatrice.

"Jake, this is not natural...this...the way we act when these people come near us. Is this magic of some kind?"

"I never gave that a thought," Jake admitted. "I don't know about magic. Maybe they've put powder in our food that makes..." He waved his hand, not willing to finish. She knew what he meant.

Not long after, two women came in and gestured for Beatrice to rise and follow them. Jake scrambled up, prepared to follow. But one of the women put a rather strong hand to his chest and stopped him.

"Where are you taking her?" he demanded.

One woman pushed on him, backing him up into the room. She smiled at him as she ran her fingers through her hair, a color similar to Beatrice's hair. Obviously, he wasn't invited to wherever they were taking her.

As he fought to calm his hard, he vowed to close his eyes the next time one of those women showed up. In the meantime, he bellowed down the hall, not even sure which way they took her. "Yell out, Bea, if you need me." He paced across the small room for what felt like an eternity.

After a long time, he heard footsteps coming down the hall. Tossing aside his sheet, forgetting to close his eyes, he ran to the door to see Beatrice and one of the women coming toward him. Eyes wide open, he saw the woman stop but gesture for Beatrice to continue. The woman gave Jake a smile, but it wasn't a seductive one.

"Bea, you okay...are you well?" he asked, unable to remember if she knew what *okay* meant. He grabbed her by the shoulders and hugged her.

She returned the embrace but stepped back and turned her head one way then another. "Look, Jake. Isn't it pretty? I have never worn my hair like a lady." She preened before him.

Relieved she'd returned safely, he stepped back to see what she was talking about. Knowing nothing of women's fashions, he asked, "They did up your hair? That's all?"

"This does not please you?" Hurt feelings flashed quickly over her face.

"Whoa! Whoa! I never said that!" He held her by the shoulders again to prevent her walking past him. "Let me get a good look."

He'd messed up. Women valued their looks, and this was the first time since Beatrice woke after all those years that she finally felt like a real woman. Jake wasn't about to ruin this for her.

His anxiety over her leaving rested now, he took time to exam exactly what the women did to her. Her hair shined, as if she stood in sunlight. They had parted it from front to back over the center of her head then braided each side, over the ears until the braids met at the back. Then a ribbon held the braids together as her hair fell in curls onto her neck and back.

"Your hair's never curled like that," he pointed out as one finger followed a twisted wave. "I like those braids." He motioned along the side of his head. "That's real pretty."

Her spirits lifted, Beatrice seemed to float into the room. "That's not all they did," she teased.

"What!" Immediately Jake feared the worst. Did someone attack her?

"One of them laid me face down and rubbed oil over me. Other knights talked of this. 'Twas used to relax sore muscles. I almost went to sleep, it felt so good." She sat on her bed and sighed, a pleasant smile on her face.

"So...you had a good time? No one...hurt...you?" There were men who would entice a woman with pleasing words then take advantage of their innocence. This, he feared, might happen to Bea when they took her away.

"'Twas a pleasant time, Jake. If such could happen to you, you might not be so grumpy," she said with an innocent expression. When he turned a deep frown on her and snorted, she fell over on her bed, laughing in rich deep tones.

Jake might have taken offense, but he caught sight of Beatrice's thigh and the underside of one rounded butt cheek. He returned to his bed and made a face at her. Which set her to laughing again. He settled for letting her think him a jester one more time.

Together didn't last the next day either. Jake checked Beatrice's neck bruises and declared them almost gone.

Once more, they sat with nothing to do.

"I thought of something yesterday when those women came in," he said as they sat shoulder to shoulder on the floor again. "A test."

He got her attention with that. "What is this test you propose?" She turned sideways to see him better.

"Well, you know how..." he rolled his hands over, hoping she could read his mind like she usually did, but this time she wasn't catching on, so gritting his teeth, he continued, "We both react to the beautiful people real strong. What if we close our eyes when they head this way? If we can't see them then maybe we won't..." That was as far as he was going. She'd have to figure out what he meant on her own.

Her eyes opened wide then she nodded. "'Tis a good plan. Will they think us strange for keeping our eyes closed?"

"Maybe but I'm tired of this. I want to get up and do something. Move. And I don't want to walk around with my..." He skipped the word. "Sticking out all the time!" He jumped up and paced from hall door to the privy door and back.

"I agree. I too feel the need to be on the move. Though I do not hurt as you do when people come, I feel like..." At this point, Beatrice lowered her head, started twisting the end of her shirt and blushed.

"If I can admit such things then you might as well finish what you were going to say," Jake admonished her. He still paced, not watching her.

"Mayhaps a man does not *feel* the same as a woman when with others," she spoke but waved her hand at his body, "but each time it is as if my body goes higher and higher, expecting something. I am prepared but never fulfilled. 'Tis shameful to say that," she said without looking at him.

"Aw, Bea." He stopped near her, aware she sat and could see his privates if he came closer. "I understand. Feeling like that ain't shameful. It's natural. When a man's body is stirred up like that, he wants to relieve himself, bury himself in a woman's body. That's the truth of it. Always has been. I guess it's the same for a woman. But we're never given a way of relieving that feeling, and that's damn frustrating."

Jake couldn't believe he'd said all that. Talking about such things was too personal.

He might have said more, but heavy footsteps came down the hall. He leaned out enough to see two men. "Time to try out that idea, Bea. Close your eyes."

She snapped her eyes closed but remained seated on the floor.

The men shot her an odd glance then ignored her. One spoke, gesturing for Jake to follow. "Uh, Bea, they want me to go with them. You going to be okay here by yourself," he held out a hand to the men, indicating they give him a minute. One nodded as Jake checked with Beatrice.

"I will call loudly, Jake, if I have need of you," she assured him.

Touching her shoulder with a gentle squeeze, he told her, "I'll be back as soon as possible."

The three headed in a new direction, going further than Jake had been so far. They entered a small room—again, one without windows. At one side was a stool and a table. Jake couldn't see what lay there because a small towel covered whatever it was. On the other side of the room was a bathing pool, smaller than the one he and Beatrice had shared. Beside that was a narrow bed piled with several towels. Several small jars sat on a table beside the bed.

One of the escorts motioned Jake to the stool then nodded to an elderly man. Like everyone else he'd seen so far, even the older man was handsome. He gritted his teeth silently as he sat uneasily on the stool. Were there no plain-looking people in this place? No one worn or bedraggled?

The older man came to Jake's side, holding a cup and brush. When he started smearing lather on Jake's face, he realized what was happening. The old man planned to give him a shave! No one had ever done that before. In a flash, he checked out the men standing around him. Clean shaven. No mustaches. No beard. No way was he letting this man shave off his mustache!

Jake ran the risk of dying right there or causing a major ruckus when he stopped the hand that approached his face with a wickedly sharp razor blade.

"Not happening," he said, his grip firm. Pointing to himself, he gestured that *he* would do the shaving, running his hand up and down his cheek. Carefully he slid his free hand up and wrapped it around the older man's hand. Holding the man's gaze, he moved his hand until the razor rested in his hand. With blade in one hand and the other palm out, he tried to assure them that he was no threat.

He could use a mirror if they had one. He held his palm up to his face and imitated shaving while looking at himself. The old man caught on quicker than the younger two. He motioned to the wall behind Jake. There hung a good-sized mirror. When Jake approached it, his image was far sharper than any mirror he'd ever used. The old man hastened to put the lather cup, a dry towel and a basin of water near at hand. Willing to keep the peace, Jake nodded, saying "Thanks."

When he finished, what he saw pleased him. A trim mustache and a narrow beard running neatly along his jaw line. The two escorts frowned, but the old man nodded with a hint of a smile. Jake winked at the elder then turned to the sour-faced two. "What's next?

Next came a haircut. The old man cut a little at a time, giving Jake the opportunity to guide him. The hair was shorter than before but still full and neater around the edges.

The elder waved him off the stool to the water. Another bath. Two in three days. He'd never enjoyed such luxury. He wondered if Bea had taken a bath as well. She never said.

The old man eventually motioned for Jake to come out of the water but handed him a towel barely big enough to cover his lap. Jake gave him a frown, but the man pulled him to the bed. Using gestures, he indicated Jake should lie down on his stomach.

Was this the oil rub Bea enjoyed so much? He saw no harm in trying it until a woman appeared at the door. Immediately he snapped his eyes shut. Then it hit him—the woman was there to rub in the oil. Damn!

He wasn't in a position to leave so he had to endure. Think of something else, he told himself, as the woman stepped up to his side. He wasn't suffering his usual distress so reasoned that closing his eyes helped. Still he had to think of anything other than the soft hands that began rubbing his shoulders and down his back, wrapping strong hands and long fingers around his ribs. Jesus! That felt good.

The woman pushed his tension right out with each stroke. She massaged his arms and fingers. Her fingers went under the small towel that covered his rear. But not too far. He relaxed enough to enjoy how she worked the muscles of his legs. His mind drifted.

He wondered if she would also rub his chest. He wasn't sure he could handle that. Apparently not because she left. The old man shook his shoulder, actually waking him up. Sitting up, more relaxed than he could ever remember, he slipped on a clean shirt the old man held out to him.

Refreshed but ready to return to Beatrice and compare experiences, Jake followed the two men out after he thanked the older man.

"Bea, close your eyes," he called out.

"You are well?"

"Right as rain." She'd never understand that so he called again, "I'm well."

Like the women did with Beatrice, one man turned back, the second stopped at the corner of the short hall and gestured Jake forward alone.

"You can open your eyes now, Bea. They're gone." He leaned against his bed, feeling more at peace than he had since before that damn war started.

Bea's gasp surprised him. She'd been sitting on her bed, but she approached him, moving her head to one side then the other, studying him. "Oh, Warrior, you are most comely." She gave him a tender smile and reached up to his face but stopped. "Your face is brighter, free of the worry you carry. I think you are happier?" She let one fingertip touch where the cheek now lay clean and smooth. Her hand gently ran over his mustache then down his beard along the jaw. "The others do not have such." She studied him then whispered, "I like this best."

He couldn't help it. Gently he pulled her to him and held her. She slipped her arms around his waist and relaxed against him. How easy it would be to love her. That truth surprised Jake. Bea was his best friend, the one he trusted with his life. The way she lived her life before...he doubted she'd ever been with a man. Her innocence soothed him. But that very innocence kept a distance between them—one she wasn't aware of.

His mind made up to embrace her as a friend, he directed her to a new subject before his will to leave her alone gave way.

The beautiful couple came early the next morning after a small woman removed the breakfast tray.

Beatrice sat on her bed, hands cupped in her lap, legs hanging off the bed, crossed at the ankles. She sat with eyes closed. Jake leaned against the bed, arms crossed over his chest, his eyes closed.

"You may open your eyes, Jacob Border." The woman spoke in English but slowly. She laughed as if she knew a joke.

"Beg pardon, but life's a bit easier for us this way," Jake said, hoping no one had a weapon out ready to kill him for such insolence.

"Life is as it is," the man said. "This worry of yours will continue. Our men wear their shafts flying proudly. You will grow accustomed to it."

"How is it that you speak our language?" Bea touched Jake's arm to maintain her balance as she slid off the bed to stand.

"We are an ancient race that has inhabited this world for time immeasurable. You are not the first beings to come to our mountain fortress. A few spoke as you do, woman." He paused then added, "Besides, we listen so we know this is your true language."

Jake wasn't about to let this man know how angry his words made him. Did they spy on Beatrice and him when they were supposed to be alone?

"Again, I say open your eyes," the woman said with a hint of demand in her tone. "Both of you. To remain as you are is unwise."

Beatrice touched Jake's arm. "I will open my eyes. You will not harm anyone."

"Bea, no," Jake said but she must have done it.

"I see only you, Warrior," she said, her way of telling him that her eyes were open but not seeing the beautiful people, therefore not enduring pangs of desire.

"I don't like this," Jake told her, his eyes still closed. Maybe that attraction thing wasn't so bad for Bea, but he'd hurt like hell.

"Warrior, look at me." She squeezed his arm tightly. "We risk harm if you do not."

Not willing to have her suffer for his stubbornness, he opened his eyes but kept them on Bea. "This is as good as it gets," he told the couple.

"Effective but useless. You shall attend us at the evening meal tonight. Others will be in to dress you appropriately." They left as quietly as they came.

"This gets stranger and stranger," Bea said, a puzzled expression on her face. "What are we expected to do this eve? And they speak our language? Others have come? Did these others get lost in that magic forest as we did? Where are they now?" She sank down on her bed, confused, eyes focused on Jake.

He threw up his hands. "Don't look at me. I can't answer anything you just asked. What bothers me—besides all the things you mentioned—is that they listen to us. How? When? All the time? In here?" He thumped the wall. "We can't even make plans to escape 'cause they can hear us."

"Escape? Can we? I have no idea where we are. And my armor? My weapons? How can I survive without them?" She asked more questions with tears in her eyes, her fingers twisting in worry.

Seeing her distress, Jake sat down beside her and wrapped an arm around her shoulder. "We have lots of questions, but those people have all the answers." On a hunch, he leaned close to her and whispered in her ear. "For now, we play along. Watch everyone. Check out this place. Maybe we can see a way to escape. We'll figure out something about your armor. Okay?"

She sat in a dejected slump next to him but nodded to show she heard and understood.

Time was their enemy. Nevertheless, for as long as they could, they could use time to find answers.

Chapter Ten
Discovery

Without the sun, they had no way to tell the time of day so were surprised when two men and two women entered their room without warning. They carried fabric, leather and sandals.

The men guided Jake to his bed where they laid out small thin pieces of fabric, a pair of sandals and several flaps of leather including a leather belt. Before he knew what they were going to do, they pulled the shirt over his head, leaving him buck-naked.

"Hey, give that back!" He grabbed for the shirt, but they pushed him away, chuckling as they did. "Bea, these fellas are a lot stronger than I took them for." He made a mistake of looking over his shoulder at her.

She stood, just as naked, her body turned away from him, but she looked over her shoulder when he spoke. "Jake, I—"

The women turned her a little more than Jake could bear so he whipped around so his back was to her side of the room. Whether it was the beautiful women dressing her—or Bea herself?—his shaft stood out proudly. He slapped away one man's hands as he attempted to wrap the short thin fabric around his waist. "Bea, these people ain't got no morals," he bitched, still fighting the two.

"This has never happened to you. Nor I, but the lady of the castle allowed handmaidens to attend her bath and dress. Perhaps it is easier for me to allow this." She grunted then squeaked. "Jake, I fear they do not wear much. This is most discomforting."

They spoke with their backs to each other. Jake finally convinced the men to show him how to put on the garment, as brief as it was while he heard Bea fussing about moving fabric around to cover parts.

"Bea, this just ain't decent," he complained when he stood assembled in short flaps of fabric, a leather belt and sandals. A flap with metal circles sewn on it covered his privates as did a smaller one that didn't cover near enough of his backside. "Ain't no way I can even turn around much less leave this room. Damnation, I ain't even got drawers to..." He refused to finish that. She was a smart woman. She'd figure it out.

"Jake," she wailed quietly. "'Tis the truth. The shirt I wore is more than this. It is beautiful but covers not my body. I fear I look like these women."

Being a contrary person at times, he gave that a few seconds of thought. "That means you're beautiful like them. Come on, lady knight. Pretend you're wearing your armor." He heard a few sniffles then a deep sigh.

"I shall try, but if I be a warrior without my armor or weapons, then you too must play the part. You must be the man I know you to be, no matter what you wear," she urged.

"Ain't gonna be easy when we turn around. We can imagine armor, my pants and coat. But the reality is we ain't wearing that."

"Warrior, we do this together."

He heard the steel in her voice, a tone that said they had

no choice. But together they could get through the evening. His sigh echoed hers as he ran his hand over his face and prayed for courage. His body already burned in embarrassment. His shaft burned with desire the minute he'd seen the two women who came for Bea. "Okay, together."

Praying he wouldn't disgrace himself in front of this strong but innocent woman, he turned slowly.

She faced him already, a slender figure wrapped in narrow grass green fabric, around the back of her neck, crossed over her breasts to cross at her back then to her front. The fabric tied and held a narrow fold that went from waist to the top of her sandals. But the fabric down the front wasn't wide enough to cover her from waist to floor. Her sides lay exposed.

So much skin burned on her until Jake thought she'd go up in flames, so great was her humiliation. Though her lack of clothing shocked him, Jake knew why his shaft quivered. Beatrice, former knight from centuries earlier, was the most gorgeous desirable woman he'd ever seen. Her lips quivered in fear even as her nipples hardened and pressed through the sheer fabric. If she felt like he did, then she'd be dripping passion between her legs.

He sensed her nervousness, her fear that he might laugh or worse, reject her. In words he'd learned from her, he gave her a gentle smile and took her hands, his eyes on her eyes, not her ravaging body. "You are the most fair and comely lady I have ever beheld."

She blushed deeper but returned his smile. "Thank you, kind sir. You forget I have seen your body when you burned with fever. *All* of your body." She did not blush when reminding him. "You are worthy of any maiden." She gave him a tiny bow.

One of the men spoke in the unknown language, pointing them into the hall. For all her courageous words,

Jake saw how nervous she was so he took her hand and slid it into the curve of his arm. He feared the unknown as well. But he figured he could handle whatever lay ahead—as long as he knew she was safe. Right now, she needed him to be strong for both of them

"Come on. Let's face this as we've done so far." No need to say more. She knew.

———

They entered a hall bigger than any Jake had ever seen. Men and women mingled at long tables and on lounges along the wall. Lounges set into cozy corners and dimly lit spaces. No more than one quick pass over the crowd confirmed: these people had no morals, few scruples about how they acted in front of each other.

The escorts led them to a long table sitting on a raised platform. Pulling out a chair for Beatrice, one woman motioned her to sit.

One of the men motioned Jake several chairs further down the table. He and Beatrice exchanged nervous glances, but he had no choice. One man motioned him to the chair while the second man took up a stance, blocking him from sitting next to Beatrice.

At least seated, no one could see how his shaft quivered. He didn't know about Bea but decided to gather information from what he could see.

No wonder he never saw windows. The entire room was actually a cavern carved out of stone. They were inside a mountain? A huge set of doors remained closed opposite his table. But Jake could see a pair of smaller doors on each side of the room. He and Bea had entered through a door behind the table. Because of its size and great height, sounds amplified until he couldn't distinguish one conversation from another. The sounds were a confusing jumble of words.

However, expressions were far easier to discern. Women seduced men with hot glances and luscious bodies that wore little cover. Men surveyed each woman as if choosing a prize horse, and every woman would be considered a valuable prize in Jake's world. No one was heavy or plain. No one was overly round. No skin was other than purest pale cream.

As for the men, even by the standards of Jake's world, this was a lusty handsome bunch. The men would slip an arm around a woman and walk her to a lounge where he simply pushed aside the gauzy material covering them and shared their bodies. Many a man didn't bother being discreet at the lounges. Jake saw plenty who sat at tables pull their leather cover up, wag their shaft at a woman who straddled his lap and bounced up and down as his mates sitting right next to him either cheered him on or got a woman of their own.

All around the great cavern men and women shared bodies in wonton abandon as if doing so was natural and expected. While Jake still sat aroused, the natural passion for joining with a woman faded. He'd caroused in brothels to be sure, but he'd never seen a casual display of sexuality on such a scale.

He wanted to catch Bea's eye and see her reaction, but then he didn't. If this sight was beyond his imagination, as worldly as he was, he couldn't imagine what she must be thinking.

The couple they first met joined them shortly after Jake and Bea were seated. The man sat next to Bea while the woman sat beside Jake. Her outfit had less fabric than anything he'd seen yet. Jake went harder immediately.

"I am Catilia," the woman informed him as several men and women brought out food. Across the entire hall, platters of food came to tables. No one ate though the noise came down considerably.

The man stood and began to speak to the people gathered there. He gestured to Jake and said his name then placed a hand on Bea's shoulder and pronounced her name, mingled in with their language.

Jake found it telling that the man called him Jake and her Bea, not Jacob or Beatrice as he'd introduced them that first time. The servants at the bath and in the hall listened well apparently and reported back.

Catilia laid a hand on Jake's leg, drawing his attention from his thoughts. "His name is Maxerim. He rules our world." She ran her hand up his bare leg but stopped shy of reaching under the leather covering his privates. Her intent was clear though. He wondered if his near-panicked expression might have stopped her. Probably not since she laughed lightly.

He had to figure out who the key players were in this place so asked, "Are you the queen?"

"I do not know this word," she said after sipping red wine. "Explain."

Oh boy, how to explain without causing a problem. Jake swallowed, hoping for a few extra moments to think. "A queen is a woman married—mated—to a king. They usually share power." He added, "But not always." He turned back to his plate of meat, odd-looking vegetables, bread, and wine.

Catilia laughed again. "We have no queen. The king can have any woman he wants and does not share power. His word is law." She cocked a sculptured brow at him and moved one shoulder so the deep blue fabric no longer covered one nipple. "Every man in here may have any woman." She gestured to a couple not far from them. The woman rode the man's lap while he suckled at her breast.

Turning back to Jake, both nipples now uncovered, she said, "Every woman here may have any man." She shot him a steamy look and added, "Including you, Jake Border."

The wine tasted sour in Jake's mouth. The meat tasted like wood. His mouth went dry, and his mind went wild. What if this King Maxerim told Bea the same thing? His heart pounded, his shaft no longer full. He tried cutting careful glances in Bea's direction, but Catilia and Maxerim blocked his view. He feared what might happen after the meal. He broke out in an anxious sweat, wondering if Bea would be subjected to the crudeness of these people.

His heart beating hard, he watched the couple push back from the table. The man spoke to several men—one who moved to Bea's side and the other to his side. While the beautiful couple stepped from the platform to mingle with the others, the two men motioned for Jake and Bea to follow them back to the door they'd come through earlier.

Jake wanted to breathe a heaving sigh of relief until he saw Bea's face. She was terrified. Panic lay in her eyes. Grabbing her hand, he once again drew it up into the bend of his arm. She clung to his side as they returned to their room. Her body vibrated. Jake knew it wasn't from passion but from abject fear.

When the men stopped at the end of the hall and allowed them to proceed alone into the room, Jake put a finger up to his mouth, warning Bea to remain silent.

Their shirts lay on their beds. Motioning for her to put it on, he turned his back to her and took off the outfit he'd worn. Slipping into his own shirt—and feeling better though his privates still hung free—he cut a quick glance over his shoulder to see if Bea was dressed. He discovered that she'd removed the flimsy outfit and left it in a pile of shimmering green fabric on the floor. As he turned, she gave the pile a vicious kick that sent it sliding to the back of the room. Seeing him dressed, she rushed to him, wrapping her arms around him, her face buried in his chest.

"Jake, that was... They were... No one paid any attention to them but us." Panic filled her every word. In his arms, she shook so hard, Jake thought she'd make herself sick.

He gathered her to him and spent a long time just holding her, giving her time to calm. Time to make sense of what she saw.

His finger to his lips again, he motioned her to silence. Leaning her against her bed—she wanted to cling to him—he pulled his mattress off his bed and motioned for her to do the same. Dragging the two toward the rear of the room, Jake sat her down on them after he pushed them together. He gathered the sheets and spread them over the mattresses. Then he went down on one knee in front of her.

Bending forward, next to her ear, he whispered, "They can hear us somehow. Best we talk about what just happened kind of quiet-like, near each other."

Bea nodded hard, scooting down under the sheet. Jake didn't hesitate to join her, passion not in his thoughts. Once down it was a matter of getting comfortable as well as being able to talk quietly together. Bea lay on her side, facing Jake. He lay on his back. He still saw panic in her eyes so he reached out, curled an arm around her and pulled her to his side. He lay flat and she still lay on her side, but Jake's shoulder was now her pillow.

He glanced down at her as she still shivered off and on. "You'll be okay," he whispered.

She disagreed, shaking her head against his arm. "No one will stop a man from taking me. I watched, Jake. I have never seen such." She buried her face but whispered, "And I do not wish to be part of it."

Now was the time for Jake to find out if she was experienced in coupling with a man. He doubted it. If she was as innocent as he suspected then tonight may have scarred her forever. He wrapped his hand around her back and over her ribs. One breast lay next to his hand. A small breast. "Bea, have you ever been with a man?"

Again, she shook her head, refusing to look at him.

"You've never seen a man and woman together?"

"Only this night. And it frightens me. Those men and women...there was no love. Is there not meant to be love of a man for a woman and woman for man before they couple like that?" She shuddered against him.

How could Jake explain that what those people did was crude sex, something with no meaning from the heart. Their lusty play was so far away from what he thought of as love.

"Bea, what you saw tonight was what men call lust. It's a normal reaction to seeing a beautiful woman. It involves no affection or desire to stay with that woman. It's just two bodies enjoying themselves. That wasn't love." He could tell she was listening.

"If that be lust then how does one know this thing called love?" She brought up her head from where she hid it and rested against his shoulder, her heart not racing as much as it was. Her breathing slower.

Jake barely remembered a girl from long ago. They were teens and had navigated a rough life for a while. They fell in love but had no home, no money. That's when Jake came up with the idea of joining the army. Before he signed up, they spent several weeks in a tiny cabin they discovered in the Pennsylvania woods. Pretending it was their home, they spent the nights making love and their days finding food.

He joined the army to discover he wouldn't train near

her. She followed him, growing great with their child. They made love as often as they could. They wanted, needed each other. He tried doing everything he could to make her happy. When they had time together, they shared their day and thoughts, hopes and dreams. That was love. He'd had it and lost it. But he remembered how it felt.

"I'm not good at explaining things like love." His mind went round and round, trying to figure it out because if he knew anything, Bea wasn't going to let this go until she understood.

"Try, Jake. Tell me so I know love when I find it," she insisted. One small fist thumped his chest. She was determined, and he was right. She wasn't going to let him get away from explaining.

"Damn it, Bea. I can't...I don't really know—"

"You do know. You told me about her."

"What the hell are you talking about, woman? I ain't never mentioned love to you." He was indignant because he'd never hurt her by bringing up someone else he'd once loved.

And then it dawned on him. What he just said to himself. His captain always called him a smart man, quick to recognize how things were and adapt to them. He and Bea had traveled for days together and for days before that as he recovered from being ill. Over the course of time, this stranger had become a friend and trusted ally. Neither wanted to hurt the other nor make them sad. They often discussed the day as they sat around an evening campfire. They never talked about the future once they realized they were no place they knew.

Jake knew two true things: he trusted Bea with his life. And that friendship he enjoyed had turned into love. He'd fallen in love, not with a knight eight hundred years out of her time. He'd fallen in love with a brave, compassionate, caring woman.

He pulled her closer by putting his other arm around her. He didn't need time to think about that, but he figured Bea might.

Bea broke into his thoughts by laying a hand on his cheek. "Fear sits heavy on me. Please tell me so I will know if a man takes me in this thing you call lust or if he takes me to love. Tell me of love like you did before."

Before? "When I was sick?"

She nodded against his arm. He turned a little closer to her, his arms still holding her in a loose embrace.

So he told her of the young woman, of their dreams of going to Texas and starting a cattle ranch near a town called Waco. He told her how they shared their lives with each other. How that friendship turned to trust and trust to love. But he ended by reminding Bea that he and the girl lived a long time ago.

"You knew this love then lost it?"

He nodded. Tired, worried about what the next day might bring, he simply held her so she could think. She worried the edge of his shirt for a long time before she said anything.

When she finally spoke, her words were the last things he expected to hear. "Jake." She folded the edge of his shirt opening, her voice timid. "My trust—my faith—in you has..." She shot a quick glance at his face, then dropped her eyes again. "You have told my story."

"Something like what happened to me happened to you?" He pulled back in order to see her better. "You never told me that." But something didn't add up. "You said you'd never been with a man. You've never seen what they do when..." He waved his hand, not willing to finish that sentence. "I'm confused," he admitted. "When did all this happen?" Maybe she fell in love with a man when she was young and never had a chance to learn about loving him. "When?"

To his surprise, she gave a sigh then reared back enough to see him face to face, less than a foot apart. She gave him a shy smile. "You told my story. Trust. Friend. Love. When? In this minute. All that you told me is you and me." She leaned over and kissed his cheek. She smiled again at his shocked expression. To show him she meant what she said, she leaned into him, eased up slowly and ran her cheek against his until her lips met his. She lit up as if a fire glowed inside of her. "Jake." She drew his name out slowly, pulling him closer, breathing him in.

His heart. His body. His soul answered her calling. Like a dam breaking loose in slow motion, tiny cracks of feelings began to seep into his body. Heat simmered. All the things Jake thought he knew—and lost—flooded through him. His mind told him this was new for Bea. Take it slow. Teach her.

But this was as new for him. He wouldn't teach her. They'd learn together. She'd seen what a man and woman could share, but she'd not experienced how that felt. The warmth that built to a fiery hot passion. That moment of pain that eased into desire. The need for one person only, to join, to share, to keep. Forever.

Jake wrapped Bea closer, his shaft so full he hurt. But this wasn't just about him. Not like the quick delight of a brothel. This was about the two of them.

Their lips met as she splayed a hand over his chest, massaging his pounding heart. He ran his hands up through her hair then curled them tenderly around the back of her neck, holding her close as they learned how to please each other.

Hands over smooth flesh. Exploring delicate ears and bright eyes. Sitting up to see, to feel. To embrace this new emotion that came so naturally to them. Soft words that turned into passionate demands. A joining so unlike what they'd seen in the huge banquet hall. Tender, hot, glorious. Demanding. Giving. Nothing held back.

His naked body covered hers, joined where a man buries himself in the ultimate gift a woman can give. His pleasure amplified by hers. Her pleasure his gift to her.

A new life. Together.

Chapter Eleven
Advice

They woke as if they'd slept together forever. No shyness. No hesitation.

Bea lay draped over Jake, her body warm and loose, though he warned her she might be sore. "Jake?"

"Humm?" He wasn't fully awake though part of him was waking quickly.

"Can we do that again? I want to feel it all. Again. Please?" She asked as she grinned and wiggled a little. She wasn't stupid. Or slow. Jake showed her ways to please him, and she used it all mercilessly.

"You sure? You might be a little sore," Jake whispered as he ran big hands over her rear that happened to be cuddling his shaft.

"Pain passed quickly last night." She slid her arms around his neck and laid her head on his chest. "I love you, Jake. There will never be pain again until one of us dies." She sighed and said quietly, "Let us pray we live long and fruitful lives." She eased his head to her and explored his face, studying his eyes. "Brown and beautiful."

"You're a handful, woman," Jake said as he nuzzled her neck. "It took a long time to realize I needed you. Not just to ease a passing itch that you could scratch." He wasn't good at saying how he felt or what he wanted. He wrapped his arms around her and for a moment prayed they'd live long enough to enjoy this feeling. "I ain't got the words, Bea. I...I love you."

The best way to make a person understand is to put actions to words. Bea and Jake renewed their commitment to each other again.

Sometime later, a foot kicked the mattress next to Jake's hand. He and Bea lay tangled in sheets, her head on his shoulder. Above him stood a woman, as radiantly beautiful as any he'd seen so far. While his body reacted, his shaft didn't demand her body.

"Bea, we have company," he said softly as he sat up, pulling the sheet over his lap.

Beside him, Bea sat as well, a bit unsteady. She fell against Jake's arm. He steadied her as she pulled her sheet higher on her chest.

The woman held another dress and motioned Bea to come to her. But Bea wasn't going. She shook her head and scooted closer to Jake. The woman motioned again, and again Bea refused.

"Jake, what if a man wants to couple with me?"

"You're not going anywhere without me."

Seeing Bea refuse, the woman left, but before either of them could relax, she returned with Catilia.

"You fear for your woman's safety?"

Jake shot the woman a fierce glance and gathered Bea closer.

"Fear not, she will meet no man. I want her to see the women's quarters."

"She's not staying there," Jake said in a dangerously calm voice.

"Of course not. You will visit with King Maxerim soon.

Both of you will return here." Catilia waved her hands to indicate their room.

"If I am to see where these women live without seeing any men then I can do this," Bea said, laying a hand on Jake's arm.

"You promise to keep her safe," Jake demanded.

"Of course," Catilia assured him.

Not willing to believe Catilia or let Bea out of his sight, Jake was torn. Bea was a warrior. But, like him, she was unarmed in new territory.

"We may do more harm by refusing her request. This we cannot afford. I shall join her then return. Ease your heart, my love," Bea whispered.

"But—"

"Peace. Trust me," Bea requested. She stood, still holding the sheet around her. Over her shoulder, she told him with a sly grin, "Between us we have no need for this sheet, but I will not give this woman the pleasure of seeing my body more than necessary."

As she moved to the bed so the escort could help her dress, Jake remarked in a dry tone, "I hate to say it, sweetheart, but that outfit isn't going to cover as much as that sheet does. You're gonna be near naked." He gave her a cheeky grin. "That won't bother me at all."

"Ever the jester," she tossed back at him as the thin fabric settled over very little of her body.

"Told you so," Jake said, one knee up, his wrist draped over it. His sheet covered his lap, disguising a shaft full of demand only for her.

"As I said, a jester," Bea cut a hot glance his way, promising pleasures to come, as the women left the room.

She no sooner left than a man showed up with an outfit for Jake. No more than was there, he needed little time to dress. Catilia said he was to meet the king. As long as he and

Bea were back in the room later, he could put up with whatever happened next.

Hours later, Jake returned to their room, only to pace. Bea wasn't there. Without the sun or some other way to tell time, he had no idea how long before she might return. He worked himself into a lather, ready to venture down the hall to look for her.

Gentle female laughter tickled his ear about the time he'd had enough of waiting. When Bea entered the room, he met her with a wide smile and quick embrace. The woman who accompanied her was as lovely as the rest but round with child. The woman clasped Bea's hands as in friendship. While Bea treated her tenderly, Jake saw worry in her eyes. Maybe things weren't as good as they thought.

Another woman with a tray—an evening tray, he figured—entered as the pregnant woman left. In fact, once the woman laid down the tray, she offered her arm as support to the mother-to-be. They strolled slowly back down the hall, leaving Jake to wonder what Bea had seen that day.

After eating they settled on the mattresses again, Jake with his back to the wall and Bea tucked in beside him. "What did you do today? Did you see any way for us to leave?" They spoke in soft voices, aware others listened.

Bea worried her bottom lip. "Catilia took me to a lovely space, very open, comfortable. Many women live there, but, Jake, they were all round with child. Every one of them." What she'd seen must have distressed her because she worried one thumbnail as she frowned.

"Sounds like a stable," Jake said.

"Truly! I have looked for a word that would explain what I saw. A stable of mares growing big with foals. Catilia walked among them, and many asked her to pray that their child would be male." Bea turned to face Jake, horror on her face. "Catilia told me that a girl child is not permitted to remain with her mother. Only males who will grow up to be guards and warriors. Those born with defects—boy or girl—are also taken from their mother. If a child grows but marred by accident, the child is removed. Don't you see? Only the perfect, beautiful ones are allowed to remain." She collapsed against Jake, a sad sigh escaping. "I have never been a mother. May never be one but I would know who the father is. These women couple with many men and know not which one fathered their child. Each one I met seemed delighted to be carrying new life, but I cannot imagine what each would think if that new life were taken from them at birth."

"Did Catilia say what they did with the babies and children that are taken away?"

"No. I did not ask."

"That goes with what I heard today," he said as he resettled her at his side, her head resting against his shoulder. "Maxerim and several armed guards escorted me around this place. It's huge, all under that mountain range where the three moons rise. Women are not permitted outside. Only guards and warriors go out. Maxerim has been outside, but it's cold, and he doesn't like it. Seems there are several exits from this place." At Bea's expectant glance, he shook his head.

"There's no way for us to find any of them if we're not allowed to move about freely. I didn't see any today, but Maxerim told me about them." He fidgeted then settled. "Honestly, I have no idea what to do. If we stay, we may be parted, and I'm not having that. Ain't no man gonna haul you off somewhere. As for the women, I don't want to play their games." He stopped and used a finger to worry his mustache.

"But you fear we may have to do as they say or suffer consequences?" Bea sat up, pulled her knees up and wrapped her arms around them. "We face a dilemma, Warrior."

She hadn't called him that in a while. Did she have a plan for breaking them out of here? Maybe that's what put her back into warrior mode.

"Can we not ask them to release us?" she pondered aloud. "They may let us go. At worst they will say no." She looked over her shoulder at him. "Either we leave with their blessings or stay and learn how to stay together in a world of lust," she concluded.

"Let's give it one more day. See what they have planned for us. Then we ask to leave or..." He waved a hand then laid it on her shoulder. "I hope for the best—"

"But fear the worse," she finished.

The next morning, two escorts, one man and one woman, arrived to escort them to Maxerim. When they entered his chamber, richly hung with furs on walls and floor, with jewel-encrusted cups and stitched cushions, they found not only Maxerim but Catilia and two other women.

Bea turned her eyes away from the sight of the king pounding himself into one of the women as she bent over a low table. The second woman stood behind the king, his garment and hers pushed aside. The woman rubbed her body up and down Maxerim's as her hands fondled the front of him, even as he buried his body in her mate.

Once the king grunted like an animal and emptied his seed into the woman, he withdrew, smacked the first woman on her naked backside then turned and pulled the second up against him. He suckled her breast as his breathing slowed.

Speaking in his language, he dismissed the women and took the damp cloth Catilia brought him. Wiping off his manhood, he shot a grin at Jake. "I can think of no better way to start a day, can you?" His privates cleaned, he motioned Jake and Bea forward.

"Open your eyes, Bea. I think he's got something important to say."

Once she opened her eyes and made sure only she, Jake, Catilia and the king were present, she relaxed enough to step up beside Jake.

Maxerim sat in a large, padded chair. Jake thought it looked like a throne. Bea would know. Catilia stood to one side, wearing a serious expression without a hint of seduction.

"You see how we live. Only the perfect may be seen. To be less so is...your word?...an abomination to us." He gestured to Jake, his eyes traveling up his body then down. "You wear hair on your face and at your shaft. We have none. It is unseemly. Your body is scarred. As a warrior, you have earned these. Our warriors avoid such, or they are never seen again."

Maxerim shifted his gaze to Bea. "This one is small, plain and carries scars as well. Her body also carries hair in places our women do not. It is untidy. Unnecessary. She has no beauty in the eyes of our men." He moved his eyes away from her, his expression one of seeing something unpleasant.

Maxerim steepled his fingers and rested his chin on them. "You, Jake, would attend only to this one woman. We do not tangle our lives with one but many. 'Tis ever our way." He stood and clasped his hands behind his back. "A few others have come up the mountain. I have told you this. You have wondered what happened to them?" When Jake nodded, he continued. "Those few stayed like you, and then we let them leave."

He saw Bea's expectant expression and finished. "Your armor and clothes will be returned to you. You will leave today. I wish you well though you are aware that beyond this place, the world is not safe."

"We've managed so far," Jake said with tight lips. "We'll be all right."

"I shall not see you again." So saying, he simply walked out of the room, Catilia several steps behind him.

Bea was so excited she squeezed Jake's hard enough to make him wince. "Give over, Bea," he said with a grin. "Will they bring our things to the room or take us to it all?"

Apparently, the escorts would take them straight to their things. With a growing sense of relief, they followed eagerly. In a small section of what looked like an armory, the escorts left them in the care of five older men, all handsome but wearing the faces of fighters. Each carried a metal staff. Jake wondered how a man could fight yet remain unblemished. He decided that wasn't his worry as he threw off the shirt and began dressing in his army uniform.

Behind him, Bea put on her leggings first then pulled the shirt over her head but left it around her neck so the material covered her breasts. She slipped her light softer chemise over her head then removed the heavier shirt. On went her padded jacket and boots with its metal. Beneath her clothes lay the pieces of her armor, complete with her weapons and shield. While the men watched without any particular interest, Jake helped her do buckles and ties.

"I am now complete," she said, turning to Jake, her helmet tucked under her right arm, her weapons in place and her shield held on her left arm. She handed Jake the two knives he'd carried.

No more words were necessary, but before they could leave, the men around them came to what looked like a kind of military attention. Catilia might not be a queen in name, but these men knew she had the king's ear. They received her respectfully. If not, fearfully.

"I shall walk with you," she said without explanation. She said something to the men and motioned Jake and Bea to follow them. She moved to Jake's left side. Bea walked on his right. They walked a long time, the path slowly going down, becoming rougher. At last, one man went ahead and unlocked a door. Metal. Maybe seven feet tall. Narrow.

The men took up position on each side of the doorway, their eyes forward. Catilia faced Jake and Bea. "They will open the door, and you will be free to leave. But I do have one piece of advice once you are outside."

The back of Jake's neck tingled. Her words sounded foreboding. He cut a glance to Bea and saw her brows drawn down into a frown. Still, freedom lay less than three feet away. Whatever advice this woman had to give would not change the fact they would be free.

The metal door was heavy. Two men had to pull it open. Outside Jake saw fresh snow. The trees were still. An odd contraption stood at the entrance outside. Jake and Bea stepped forward into freedom. Bea closed her eyes and sucked in a deep breath of cold fresh air.

One man took a step out of the door and rapped his staff against the metal ball several times. The clarion sound vibrated through the area.

Jake turned to face Catilia who stood just inside the doorway. Several men had their staffs pointed toward Jake and Bea while the other men had hands on the door ready to close it. "That advice?"

"You now join the babes and children. Unlike those who nourished the beasts of this mountain, you will not die immediately. You will live long enough to give them a fight. My advice? *Run.*" The door slamming shut cut off her insanely wicked laughter.

Chapter Twelve
No Purpose

"Warrior, to me," Bea yelled. "We make for the tree line, find protection among those boulders." She pointed to a large stand of trees growing at the side of the mountain.

While Jake talked to Catilia, she'd been scouting a way out of the place. Jake fell into step behind her as they raced across a small clearing. Once among the trees, they took up position among boulders, large ones at their backs.

Even as they stood guard, prepared for they knew not what, Bea spoke, "She truly is a vile woman. Do you believe her? About the children?"

"Afraid so, Bea," Jake said. He pointed back the way they came. "Look there. Cloth. A small blanket. A shirt."

Bea gasped. "They remove girl children, the sickly, and plain ones then toss them out here as a sacrifice?"

"Looks that way, the bastards!"

"We know not what to expect, Jake. We are not defenseless babes or young ones. We have a better chance of getting out of these mountains."

"I don't hear or see anything. How about moving

further down? If we can get off this mountain we can hightail it away."

"If that means *move* then I agree. I have the armor. That will slow down whatever may come. Cover the back trail."

Jake nodded, and she moved out. From tree to tree and boulder to boulder, they moved on thirty feet before Jake pulled her to a stop. "Do you hear that?" He cocked his head to one side and closed his eyes. "Sounds like water. Maybe a waterfall? Sounds like a lot of water." He scanned the area. Seeing nothing threatening, he motioned her forward.

"Damn!" Jake and Bea stood at the edge of a cliff maybe two hundred feet high. Across from them, water poured over the edge, tons of water, roaring as it fell. Below them though lay huge rocks. To fall from this ledge would mean death, not a possible watery escape.

Pulling her back, he motioned to the left. "Let's see how far this goes. Maybe we can head away from it."

She moved forward, her sword out, her shield up for protection. They ran in a crouch, avoiding anything that might make noise. The cliff edge on their right went on and on. They stopped and took a knee, breathing hard.

"That's got to be a river running along down there, damn it," Jake fussed. "How about cutting straight through the trees? We have to get away from this cliff. It gives us no place to go in case of trouble."

Bea nodded and headed away from the river's high edge. "We must take care that we do not approach any of those guards," she said softly.

They hadn't gone more than a hundred yards before a roar blasted through the area. An animal roar. Off to the left. Jake put a hand over Bea's shoulder, gesturing to veer away. Another roar, louder and closer, came from in front of them.

"You see anything?"

Bea shook her head but went back to scanning the area. "Look! I think I saw something just beyond that stand of trees," she whispered and pointed.

Something moved to their right, making a thudding sound. A similar sound came from their left. Another roar came from in front of them. Out of the day's brassy glare padded the biggest damn cat Jake had ever seen. Like the huge butterfly—totally out of proportion to what he knew—this cat was perhaps twenty feet tall and forty long from nose to the end of its twitching tail. Its small ears lay back along its head. The lips around a mouth filled with a double row of jagged teeth pulled back, leaving a series of frown lines between mouth and forehead. If this had been a situation other than life or death, Jake would have loved having a white cat with a pattern of black squares along its body and legs. Its paws were the size of one of Jake's army tents. Pure white fur covered its chest.

The big cat in the front sat with a decidedly heavy thump, its mouth open, displaying teeth as long as Jake's arm. That gorgeous tail switched side to side.

Lost in wonder at what they saw, neither noticed that the other two had moved up closer. The three effectively cut off their escape. The only way out now was the cliff edge.

The leader stood, his tail still, his head low, his eyes drilling the humans in front of him. He took a step forward.

Jake and Bea stepped back two. "Bea, we have to split up. I'll draw them off while you get outta here." He dare not lose eye contact with the predator casually stalking them.

"Together, Warrior. I said I would follow you. I break not that promise now," she breathed at his side. "I have not told you today that I love you, Jake. You know this, but I like saying it." Though her words came out through a set of chattering teeth, she still said it.

"Together, Bea. Forever," Jake promised.

Back-to-back they stood, the trio of cats pushing them. Jake took a second to note how close they were to the edge. His heart sank. They would not survive an attack by the giant cats. Nor would they survive a fall.

With thirty feet to go, he saw steel straighten Bea's spine. He knew instinctively what she would do. What her kind of fighter would do. What his soldiers would do if they had their backs to the wall. They'd pull up battle courage and attack. The odds of survival were nothing, but they'd die fighting rather than being pushed off a damn snowy cliff.

"To me, Warrior," Bea screamed as she raised both sword and shield. A small streak in shining armor raced toward the center cat. Jake could not refuse her call or give her less than his best. He roared like the big cats and followed her lead.

The cats dodged the sword and staff, continuing to drive the two back. Back and even more until Jake and Bea stood three feet from the cliff's edge. It mattered not how close they were now.

Jake bled from deep wounds along his side, arm and one leg. Bea's helmet came off when one giant paw missed her chest and rolled her protection off her head. She bled from her ears, proof that the battering the cats gave her caused injuries even under the armor.

She lunged and managed to bury her sword in one cat's chest. Though it faltered, a great paw came out, hitting her so hard she flew off the cliff.

"Bea!" Jake went mad. The one thing that made his life worthwhile had just perished. With a roar, he bellowed, "Together!" just as the leader grabbed his body, shook it like a rag, and tossed it up. The cat misjudged where Jake would land if the animal expected a meal. Jake landed at the edge of the cliff, rolling. He wasn't conscious when his body went over the edge.

Two bodies lay on ragged rocks at the bottom of the cliff. Bones pulverized. Blood from a hundred places. Sword and staff near but no longer needed. Their deaths served no purpose.

But Fate wasn't through with them.

Chapter Thirteen
Jake's Journey

Weird dreams played with Jake's mind. Images. Odd sounds. A woman but not like any he'd ever seen. A sword? A cat. A *huge* cat. His head hurt from all these things.

The day came though when the images and sounds slid into the background, replaced by men's voices. A woman's voice now and then. Not the one in his dreams though. But then, those weren't real.

Gradually he woke, hurting in a few places. Sore. His head pounding. For a few minutes, he remembered such headaches. But whatever memories those were faded.

He lay on a bed. Sunlight brightened the back of his closed eyes. His mouth was dry, but someone held a wet cloth to his lips and squeezed a few drops of water into his mouth. *Nectar.* What the hell was *nectar*? He let sleep take him once more.

The next time sunlight shone on him he managed to open his eyes, blinking against the soft warm yellow beams. The sunlight seemed odd, he thought.

"Welcome back, Sergeant," came a deep voice at the side

of Jake's bed. "You've been quite ill. In fact, I wasn't sure you'd ever wake up."

For some reason, Jake remembered something similar. Maybe this man had said it.

"What happened?" Jake had to pause a few seconds and catch his breath, maneuver his dry mouth. "Where am I?"

"I'm Doctor Mayfield. You're in a hospital in southern Pennsylvania. You've been here two months. I can say with all honesty I've never had a patient who lived this long, coming in and out of consciousness. With that head wound and four other wounds, you should have died in that forest where your men found you."

At this point, Jake laid still, arms at his side, pain there but tolerable for now. Confusion warred with an attempt to explain where he was with where he thought he was.

"The war?"

"Lee surrendered to Grant at Appomattox in April. You were wounded a day before that, but it took three more days for your men to find you. I don't know how you survived. But those men never gave up. They saved your life."

At this point, Jake was thirsty, hungry and worn out. He must have looked haggard. The doctor reached out and checked the bandages around his head and several on his chest and shoulder.

"For the severity of those wounds, you seem to be doing better. I'll leave you in Mrs. Woods' hands for now." The doctor patted Jake on the shoulder then left. As he moved away from the bed, Jake saw a tiny woman standing with hands clasped, watching him.

While he watched her, she moved a stool up close to the bed and sat. Her hair was autumn red, and her eyes were gray. She wasn't young, a grandmother perhaps. She dipped a cloth into water and leaned forward. "Your lips will feel better if I wet them. May I?"

Almost asleep, Jake managed a small nod. The cloth felt like heaven against his mouth. Some of the water dribbled over his lips. He couldn't remember anything that tasted so good. He sighed, ready to sleep more. But the woman next to him brought him awake unexpectedly.

"As you have said, that tastes like nectar, I imagine." She wet the cloth again, this time letting more water trickle into his mouth.

"I don't...what's *nectar*?" As sleepy as he was, Jake couldn't rest until he figured out why this unknown word was important.

Mrs. Woods smoothed hair off his forehead and touched his cheek with a small work-worn finger. "According to you, nectar is the finest thing you've ever had to drink," she smiled as she spoke. A sad sort of expression settled on her face as if one just finished an excellent story, knowing another such tale would never come along again.

"I don't know that word," he managed to say as his eyelids grew heavy.

"Rest now, Sergeant. You've lived a great story. Soon I can share it with you."

"How is the patient this morning, Mrs. Woods?" The doctor sat on the stool she'd vacated so he could examine Jake.

"He wakes for longer periods. He's eaten and taken plenty of water. The orderly helped him to the water closet so he's stronger."

Doctor Mayfield sat back and caught Jake's gaze. "Those bandages on your chest will come off soon. I left them on while you were so sick, tossing and turning. I must say, you had vivid dreams...or nightmares...while you were unconscious. Mrs. Woods can tell you more about that than I can."

The doctor started to move away but left final instructions with the woman. "His commanding officer, a Captain Richmond, is coming to see him this afternoon. The orderly will be here soon to clean him up. Do you think he's strong enough to sit in the garden?"

"Thank you for letting me know, Doctor. The sergeant is an unusual patient. I appreciate you letting me sit with him." She paused and shot a glance at Jake. "He may say he's strong enough to walk out of here right now. I believe he could be quite stubborn, but the truth is, he's not strong enough yet to get out of bed and sit outside. Maybe in a few days." She clasped her hands in front of her and dropped her gaze, aware Jake heard her.

"Very well. The captain can visit Sergeant Border here." With that, he left, and the woman returned to her stool where she sat as Jake fumed.

"Who the hell are you to say that about me?" he demanded, agitating the pain in his chest and setting his head to pounding again.

The woman sat up straighter, looked him right in the eyes and introduced herself in a stern voice. "My name is Melissa Woods. I'm sixty-nine years old. I lost my husband, both sons and a grandson in that damn war. You remind me of my oldest son, Adam. I'm not about to let you kill yourself by being stubborn. When you're well enough to leave, you and I will part company. *You'll* probably be glad to get rid of me, but *I'll* not be forgetting you any time soon." The lady sat like a red-headed general who'd just issued orders that were to be followed and not questioned.

And that's what happened. "Yes, ma'am," Jake said quite humbly, recognizing a commanding figure even if she was a woman.

"I've sat with you since the day they brought you here," she continued. "Though you were unconscious, you talked.

You'd rest then talk more. It didn't take me long to realize you were telling a story. An unbelievable one. That first night I returned to my room and wrote down everything you said in a journal. Afterwards, I brought that with me and wrote as you talked. You'd rest, still horribly sick, but then you'd begin again. I can't imagine what nightmares must have been in your mind this entire time." She cupped her hands in her lap and gazed out the big window behind Jake's bed.

"Not all of your story is a nightmare. Certainly enough to keep a sane person awake in the dark, wondering what might come next." She lowered her eyes to meet his. "Parts of your story are beautiful. Amazing. And intimate. I might have blushed as I wrote what you said, but I knew that if you survived, you'd want to read that journal. And," she shrugged tired shoulder, "if you died, I would bury the story with you. It's a tale your heart had to tell, but no one else need ever know," she promised.

"When can I see this story?" Jake's head still pounded, but the woman had his attention.

"When you are strong enough to sit in the garden, I will read the story to you." She frowned at him and issued a warning. "*I* will determine when you are ready." She snorted and rolled her eyes. "You would lie to me."

Jake gave her a deep frown. "I ain't never lied to no woman," he defended himself.

At which Mrs. Woods nodded in agreement. "I believe you, Sergeant. But as in your story, there is always a first time for everything."

An orderly came up about then. "I got orders to get the sergeant ready for a visitor."

"I shall leave you to it then, Private. Take care," she shot a warning glare at the young man. "His captain will be displeased if his best sergeant is not in top shape."

Jake sucked in a chuckle when the soldier saluted her, caught himself doing it, and got flustered. He shifted from foot to foot as the woman stood and pushed the stool to the head of the bed.

"Behave yourself," she told Jake but winked at him. She passed the private and gave him a fierce glare.

An hour later, she returned, escorting Captain Richmond. "I'll leave you to visit, sir," she said sweetly, a side of her that Jake had yet to see.

The captain took the stool, and the men shook hands. "I have to say, Sarge, I thought you'd either die during the trip or after they left you here. If we were still fighting, we probably wouldn't be having this conversation." The man smiled and settled on the stool, leaning forward, arms resting on his legs, hat and gloves in hand.

"Where do I report when I'm released, sir?"

"Border, you lay near death for days before your men found you. I've learned you damn near died several times while here. The colonel's been keeping tabs on you. He said to tell you that you've done good things in this man's army, but it's time that you retire. I think you had a birthday sometime during the spring that makes you fifty-one. Not that you probably couldn't handle army life again, but—"

"—the colonel doesn't think I can keep up any more," Jake finished. He had wondered what his options would be when he healed. Now he knew. "When?"

"We won't discharge you until you are completely healed. You have the monies you've saved over the years. That ought to help you get established somewhere. And the army owes you for the time you've been here. Frankly, Sarge, I can't imagine not having you around. You certainly kept me on the straight and narrow path to promotions during the years. I wish you the best of luck, Sergeant Border." The captain stood and shook Jake's hand. Turning smartly, he left, tipping his hat to Mrs. Woods as he did.

Jake expected her to return to his side the minute the man left, but she caught his eye, nodded solemnly and left the big room.

What was he going to do? The only real life he'd ever known was the army. Now he was too old and feeble to be part of that apparently. He turned his face to his pillow and gave in to grief.

Mrs. Woods did not return that day. Jake could honestly say he didn't miss her. He still mourned the end of his army career. As to what would come next, he wasn't worried about it. Maybe in days to come as he recovered well enough to get around on his own he might give it some thought. For now, he needed help simply standing long enough to take care of his bodily needs. If he'd ever had a spark for living, it seemed to have faded out.

His eyes opened the next morning to see the woman sitting quietly at his side. She was reading, and he wondered if it was the journal she'd talked about. He attempted to sit higher in bed, perhaps get the private's attention so he could take a piss.

He shouldn't have worried. The private showed up at his side as if by magic. The old woman stood aside for them to pass. When he returned, she stood at the big window at the head of his bed, a dreamy look on her face. Jake couldn't avoid a grunt of pain as he sat at the edge of his bed.

"Would you prefer to sit up a while, Sergeant?" Mrs. Woods didn't turn but did ask.

"Yeah, I'm about tired of lying down and," he fiddled

around with the covers, "I'm tired of being tired," he admitted.

The woman left his side and the room but returned shortly with several pillows. "These will cushion your back some but may not be so comfortable after a while," she said as she held two pillows against the iron rail headboard while he managed to scoot into position. "Well done," she said with an easy smile. She picked up a leather-covered book from the stool and resumed her seat. "You make remarkable progress each day, Sergeant Border," she complimented.

"You might as well call me Jake. As soon as the doctor releases me, the army will too. The captain left the impression I'm a bit too old and beat up to be any use to the army now that the war's over."

"Then you may call me Melissa. We are now even, Jake. Not sure what to do with ourselves." She held the book carefully, her focus once more on the sun outside his window.

"How come, ma'am?" Jake waved his hand at her. "You lost your men folk, but surely you have a home somewhere."

"Home? It's burnt to the ground outside Atlanta. I traveled here to help my husband. He signed up with the northern army. He was a doctor."

"How did a man from the south come to join the north?"

"We never owned another human. We believed men—and women—should be free to choose their life's way. By the time we traveled here, our oldest son had joined the army of the south. Adam had his own home in Mississippi. Our youngest, Thomas, followed his brother. Both died. Our grandson, David, lived in Texas, near a place called Waco." She gave him a speculative look. "You have dreamed of going to Texas. To this town." She didn't ask him. She said it as if she knew for sure. "David died just like his father and uncle, but he wore blue. Could be they may have met on a battlefield somewhere." She sighed.

"What about Doctor Woods? You said he died?"

"He worked himself to death. So many men flooded this hospital. So much to do. He wouldn't stop. Or even slow down. He wasn't letting one of the boys die if he could prevent it." A single tear slipped down a thin cheek. "An orderly found him one morning, slumped over a patient he'd attended. A man much like you—someone with little chance of surviving. The man died, and my husband died with him." She shook herself, perhaps shaking off memories. "I stayed on at the administrator's request. I do not nurse the sick. I sit with them when hope is gone." She gave Jake a sad smile. "And so I have been at your side, praying you would survive. It seems my prayers were answered."

She cocked her head to one side and frowned. "More importantly, I believe I was meant to be here. To listen to the tale you've told. Oh, none of it's true," she said, waving a hand as if pushing that possibility aside. "But imagine if it had been. The wonder of it. The adventure. The surprises and tragedies of such a tale. If nothing else, Jake, you could take up a pen and create stories to entertain."

She studied him for a few seconds then shook her head. "No, I think this tale came from your heart, not your imagination." She held up a hand to ward off whatever he wanted to say. "Once you hear this story, you can tell me what *you* think."

She left it at that. No matter what Jake said to entice her to begin reading the story, she refused. "When we are alone in the garden, I will share." She gave him a cheeky grin before rising. "You will heal faster if you must wait. But do not think to cheat. I'll know better. I have a few errands to attend, Jake. Enjoy the golden sunlight. Be glad it's not a constant brassy color," she ended.

What the hell does that mean, Jake wondered. The orderly came later and helped him settle for a nap. And in his dreams, Jake saw three moons followed by brassy-colored midday sunlight.

Several days later, the doctor—and Melissa—pronounced him well enough to go into the garden. Still too weak to walk to the far side of the place, to a bench beneath a tree, he put up with the orderly taking him out in a convalescent wheelchair.

Once settled, Jake couldn't wait for Melissa to begin. She hesitated though. "You said you'd read the story. What are you waiting for?" He rubbed the arms of the chair, back and forth, not sure why he was so anxious.

"Because of that," she said and pointed to what he was doing. He immediately stopped. "I think you're worried about what I might read. It's a story, Jake. I'm not sure how you came up with it and..." She stopped and gazed out over the flowerbeds, a calming sight after the torn-up lands she'd heard about from patients. Sucking in a big breath of air, she studied his face. "I'm not sure how you will take this. It's pure fantasy, but after getting to know you, how you act and speak and react to things, this is *your* story. This man is *you*." She rubbed the dark leather of the journal where it lay in her lap. "The question is...who is this woman?"

Her words left Jake with his mouth hanging open. "Is the story that bad?" He wasn't sure if he wanted to hear it or not now.

Melissa reached out and took his hand in her smaller wrinkled one. "Oh no, Jake, this is a wonderful tale. I think," she squeezed his hand hard, "that you *must* hear it. I think it's important though I can't imagine how or why. Does that make any sense?"

Jake was honest with her. "Not really but maybe it will as you go along."

"Very well then. Let us begin this fascinating journey." Melissa opened the journal and turned several pages before she explained. "You talked off and on the first day you arrived. Several hours passed before I realized you weren't talking about the war itself but being lost and unable to find your way back to your men. I entered your name on the first page here and your condition. Honestly, at that point, few expected you to live. I added my name as the recorder, meaning what I wrote here wasn't my story. The first night I returned to my room and found this empty journal among my husband's things. I wrote what I could remember. I added the date each day. The story ended the day you woke up and decided to live. I think that's important to remember, Jake." She cleared her throat with a delicate cough and began Jake's remarkable story.

I'm lost, dying. My head hurts so bad. My whole body hurts. I gotta find my men. I can't even hear cannons any more. This damn forest is thick and odd looking. I fell. Hard to get up. I feel faint, like those ladies who watch battles from the ridges and faint at the sights and sounds of battle. But they still insist on watching. I pitch face first beneath a tree. Hard to breathe. Hard to move. I feel something metal. A boot? That makes no sense. When I manage to turn over, I think I might have screamed like one of those fancy ladies. A statue or something sits on a rock, slumped like he's asleep. Metal covers his body, head to boot. My heart! It's pounding so hard it makes me bleed more. But I'm not alone. I'm dying but not alone. I pull closer though my pain is agonizing by now. Is the boot soft enough to hold my head as I die? Maybe. But I won't be alone. I don't want to be alone.

Melissa stopped and closed the journal. Once again, she rubbed the leather as she waited for Jake's reaction. She cut her eyes to him, studying him.

"A man of metal?" Jake looked like he'd been hit with a club. "I truly was dying, imagining that." He tried to laugh off what he'd heard but couldn't put any humor in the sound. "What does that mean?" He leaned toward Melissa. She knew the whole story. She could give meaning to what he just heard.

But she wasn't going to satisfy his curiosity. She wrapped a leather strap around the journal and slipped it back into the deep pocket of her white apron. She sat silently, watching him.

When he finally realized she would neither read more nor speculate on what she'd read, he slumped in the chair. "I'm a little worn out now. Maybe that guy can wheel me in." He didn't look at her or thank her. His mind sought to reconcile dying with a man of metal. There was more story to come. Who was the metal man?

In his dreams that night, he saw a strange forest and a huge tree, but details after that eluded him. He wanted more. More of his story.

For a week, Jake and Melissa sat beneath an oak while she read to him. Time within his story passed in agonizing slowness. Jake described the man waking up to a sword at his throat. How this metal man had cared for him after he died then came alive again.

That part baffled both of them.

"How can that man die then come alive again? That makes no sense." He waved a hand at her. "I agree with what that guy said...he just fainted. He didn't die."

"But this man in the metal suit with the long sword swears the man died. He saw the man no longer breathing," Melissa reminded him. "I don't know, Jake. I just wrote down what you said. The story flows from one thing to another in good order and is entertaining." She grinned at him. "Without fever, no man would ever tell how he wore so little while lying under a cape."

Jake frowned at her as he snorted. "Damn right. That ain't polite for a lady to hear."

"That may be but it's your story, and that's what the soldier said." She couldn't quite keep a smile off her lips.

"It ain't funny, woman," Jake growled.

"Now that right there makes me more certain that this man who is recovering is you." She pointed a finger at him then thumped the journal. "That's exactly the kind of thing this man says." She gave him a cheeky grin that lit up her face. "Makes you sound grumpy. In here," she held up the journal, "and in there," pointing to the hospital.

Jake had no answer for that but a disgusted snort.

The day came when they walked to the bench beneath the tree together. Jake's injuries were healing nicely. Melissa hinted that he might be released soon. She also hinted that a critical part of Jake's story was coming up.

He already knew that the knight—the man in the metal armor—decided the two should be moving on. The soldier wanted to find his army unit, and the knight wanted to return home. However, Melissa stopped reading when the knight said he had something important to tell the soldier.

Something that might change his willingness to travel together.

By now in the story, both Jake and Melissa realized that the two had bonded as companions. Both warriors. Jake remarked how familiar that sounded...that word *warrior*.

When Melissa finished reading for the day, the two often sat and discussed what she'd read so far. She made it a point never to agree or disagree with what Jake thought. He called her on it one day.

"You know the whole story. Yet you won't say anything that gives me a clue where this damn thing is going." He thumped the cane he used against the side of the bench. "You're a mean bitch at times." Realizing he'd just insulted a woman old enough to be his mother, one who'd been nothing but kind to him and a friend by now, he hung his head, sighed and apologized. "Sorry, I didn't mean that. You've been real good to me. You didn't deserve what I just said."

She sat a few seconds then replied, "I accept your apology. You've said that very thing, by the way—being a bitch—before." Again, she touched the journal, "but you didn't apologize then. I can hardly wait to read *that* to you." She gave him a serene smile that set Jake to growling.

The next day Melissa opened the journal but sat still rather than read.

"You're awful quiet." Jake pointed out the obvious. "Bad things coming up in the story?"

Melissa shrugged. "Depends on you, I suppose. I saw this next part as wonderful. Amazing. A test for you...I mean, the man you talked about."

"How so?"

"This part of the story tests how strong the soldier is. This is a different kind of challenge that almost all men would throw aside."

"Ain't like this guy's not been challenged before. Like me..." He stopped as if that character was him rather than a dream. "Everyone faces challenges. I have." He waved a hand at Melissa. "You have for certain. And lost more than I ever have." He reached over and took one of her hands in his, giving it a gentle squeeze. "You're a brave woman, Melissa Woods. Don't let anyone ever tell you different." He felt good telling her that.

"Thank you, Jake. Your words ease my heart. But you must be brave when I read today," she warned as she opened the journal. Cutting her eyes at him then back to the story, she began.

While we wait for your side of the story, can you at least tell me your name?

The knight hung his head. I have no name. It was taken from me.

"So this guy pissed off the metal man but didn't worry that the man might kill him?" Jake sat forward, arms on his legs. "That's some kind of trust," he observed.

"Indeed. And that trust will be tested soon."

Jake nodded and sat up so he could watch Melissa as she read.

What year was this great battle of yours?

1865. Why?

The man staggered, in shock. 'Eight hundred years, Warrior. I sat on this rock for eight hundred years.'

The soldier eased away. Eight days made sense but eight hundred years? This man was ill clearly.

I am alone, the metal man said. And your name, Warrior?

Jacob Border—friends call me Jake.

A gasp and Melissa nodded. Jake shook his head in defiance. "You named yourself, Jake. That is why I said I was glad to be sitting with you. I wrote this down as a story that you told, but..." She gave him a penetrating look.

He held up both hands toward her, warding off the implication of her unspoken words. "I'm not crazy, and neither are you. We both know that was just talk while I was sick." His heart raced, and his mouth went dry. A shiver of fear ran down his spine. He'd named himself in a dream. A dream that meant nothing. Or shouldn't mean anything. But he had a funny feeling this was more than a dream, even if he wasn't about to admit that out loud.

"What's this guy gonna say next?" He feared the next few minutes. How could a simple story affect him like this? Then again, maybe it wasn't so simple.

My tale will scare you. You must be brave for it is a tale of magic and dishonor. I broke a sacred code, was found out, and punished. I have no land, no people, no name. I am alone, said the knight.

No, no you're not. We're here. Together.

Let us begin with the hardest part, the knight said. The man raised his hands and slowly removed his helmet to reveal eyes the color of storm clouds in a face as soft and delicate as pink petals.

You're...you're... The soldier's mind had trouble changing who he thought was a man into a woman with smooth skin, pink lips and rich brown hair.

You may say it aloud, Warrior. Be brave, she encouraged with a dejected look on her face.

You're a woman! How had he missed that? You lied to me, he shouted in anger.

Melissa finished the day's reading at the point where the knight...the woman...told Jake she would explain why she allowed him to think her a man.

Journal closed, Melissa sat back against the bench and heaved a sigh that lasted a long time. She said nothing, giving Jake time to grapple with this revelation.

"How could I possibly dream up all that? It's a goddamn fairy tale," Jake moaned.

"Have you ever seen a knight? Or even a picture of one?" Melissa asked as she reached into one of her apron pockets. When Jake shook his head, she handed him the paper. "I found a book in a friend's library. He's far older than me and not part of the world much anymore. He taught history at a university in New York then retired here for peace and quit." Jake snorted at that while she stuck out her tongue and blew a nasty sounding noise. "I asked about knights, and he showed me this picture. He let me use paper and pencil to trace the likeness. You can easily see why the lady knight could have fooled you."

He took the paper and whistled in amazement. "You can't see anything but armor." He ran a finger over the pieces covering arms, legs and head. The knight held a sword almost as long as he was tall. On the left arm, he held a shield. "How could they maneuver in all that?" He moved his own arm freely, amazed by how a knight could be so weighted down. "These men must have been strong, powerful."

"When Europe was at its mightiest, men such as this one and the one in your story guarded kingdoms and protected the people who lived there. So, for your knight to have sat on that rock as she said, for eight hundred years, meant her world had passed from existence. Can you imagine how that must feel," Melissa said, wonder in her voice.

"But it's only a story. Something I made up while..." He

clamped his mouth closed, more and more worried that he was crazy.

Another week passed. Jake could function on his own but slowly. Melissa came in one morning, an air of concern radiating from her.

"What's ruffled your feathers," Jake joked as he tugged on his boot. He stood but groaned. The shoulder wound still bothered him.

"The doctor will be in shortly. Best you wait until you hear what he has to say before we go outside." The day threatened rain. "Looks like a dreary day for news."

Jake had expected news for the last several days. When the doctor released him, the army would too. He'd known this day would come, but while he was so injured, he'd put off thinking about what would...could...come next

He sat back down on his bed, prepared for the news. Whatever the doctor had to say wouldn't surprise him, but what Melissa said did.

"When you leave, I'll leave as well."

"Huh? Where are you going?" Jake's mouth hung open. He imagined this rough but compassionate woman staying around, helping those who most needed help.

"To Texas. When my grandson moved to Waco, he got lucky. Met a man who had a nice cattle ranch. Not a big place but comfortable-like is how David described it in his letters. He said Grant Stone made it a nice place to live and work. David was passionate about the ranch. Grant died peacefully about a year after they met. He willed the ranch to David. It's not the biggest one around but no small business either." Melissa moved to the window where she sometimes stood, her thoughts miles away. "Before David left to join the northern army he sent us his will, leaving the ranch to his father and me."

She turned to Jake. "I own a cattle ranch hundreds of miles from here and have no idea how to run it. I have no other home than that now. I suppose I could say I'm lucky, but that place came to me by way of two deaths...my grandson and my husband." She took a seat on the stool and clasped her hands in her lap.

Her position reminded Jake of the knight in his story. Her name was Beatrice. That's how his dream said the soldier found her, sitting with her hands in her lap.

By now in the story, the two had hunted for strange but tasty rabbits and fought a giant butterfly. When Melissa stopped reading the day before, the two had discovered that the world they thought they knew wasn't their world at all. This one had three moons and daylight that was brassy colored instead of soft yellow. The soldier even tried to choke Bea he was so scared.

Melissa stopped reading when the soldier and Bea, as he called her, fought men with long pike-like staffs and were captured. Melissa was near the end of the journal. Maybe his time here and the story would end at the same time.

In the meantime, he watched Melissa. To his surprise, he saw tears creeping down her cheeks. Reaching out, he gathered her hands in hers. Hands quite small. Fragile.

"Hey, don't cry. You'll do fine out there on that ranch."

"You don't believe that any more than I do." She swatted his hands then held on to them again.

That's how Doctor Mayfield found them.

Jake patted his bed and pulled Melissa over to sit by him. It might be the end of one part of his life, but after what she said, it seemed the end for Melissa as well. She was upset, but he had a feeling she was more upset about him than herself.

The doctor plopped down on the stool and slumped for

a minute. "We're still receiving wounded. I've been in surgery since breakfast." That explained what looked like blood on his white jacket. Those drops and spray *were* blood.

"Sergeant, I'm releasing you day after tomorrow. I understand the army is releasing you as well. It's a damn shame. You give decades to the bastards, and they calmly say enough. Goodbye." He held out his hand. "I'm glad you lived, Border. Glad to have met you. Best of luck." With a heavy sigh, the doctor heaved his body up and left the room.

Jake and Melissa sat side by side, their shoulders touching. He had no idea what was going through her mind, but his was almost blank. The only thing he could think of was collecting his pay and the money he'd saved over the years then... That was as far as he could think.

"Guess I know when I'm not wanted," he tried joking. He too heaved a weary body up and held out a hand to his companion. "Come on, you lazy old woman. Let's see where these two end up today. Divide what's left in half, and we'll finish tomorrow."

"Lazy, my ass," Melissa muttered as she grasped Jake's hand and hauled herself up to stand at his side. "If that soldier and that knight can keep moving then so can I." As she moved ahead of him to the door, he heard her mutter something similar, but he didn't catch it. Shaking his head, he followed her to their bench.

Later, turning his head away from Melissa, Jake blushed a fiery red as she read about the soldier and Bea taking a bath together. What she read sounded so much like what he would say that it was impossible not to say that he was the soldier in the story though pages earlier the soldier had named him such.

Melissa pointed out something, reminded him of the day he called her a *mean bitch*. "See, I told you that you'd said that before." She chuckled and teased him, "I said I'd enjoy reading *that* part to you."

"Ain't funny at all," he grumbled, his face still turned away. Probably didn't help as he figured his neck even burned from embarrassment.

"Oh, things get even better," she warned him, laughing aloud.

"Give me that damn journal then. I'll read it for myself." He reached out to take it from her, but she slapped his hand hard and put the journal behind her back.

He wasn't going to fight an old woman for a book filled with an improbable story that embarrassed him to death. "Get on with it then, but try not to enjoy it so much," he warned.

She read, coming to a part where the soldier realized he had fallen in love with Bea. The world they found themselves in centered around people who were more beautiful than anyone imagined. Melissa managed to keep a straight face as she read about the soldier's physical reaction to the gorgeous women. It didn't help that she also read about a similar reaction that Bea suffered.

They both laughed at Bea's reaction to having wrinkled fingers from being in the bath so long.

Neither laughed though when the dream continued into what both considered the nightmare affair of clothing and suffering through the meal in the huge hall where morals and discreetness had no place.

Jake stopped her, a shocked expression on his face. Eyes wide, mouth open and shaking his head. "What kind of people are they? That's indecent. Damn. And that poor woman. She's never been in a place even remotely like that." He stood, stomped around then paced. "That poor man. How does he save her?" he questioned.

"They find comfort in each other, Jake," Melissa told him before she started reading again.

"I'm glad. Glad they found each other," Jake finally said. He leaned his arms on his knees and studied the grass. "That part about the girl and Texas. Yeah, that's me. That was a goal I set a long time ago. But like this," he waved at the journal, "it's all a dream. That woman, that knight Bea that I dreamed up." He smiled at Melissa. "I could have loved a woman like that." He reached down and pulled several pieces of grass that he started braiding together. "Together. I hope the story ends well for them," he said as he focused on the wild lawn and blooms.

"We'll finish tomorrow. We should prepare to leave the next day. The trip will be long." She stood, slid the journal into her apron pocket, and brushed wrinkles out of her skirt.

It took Jake a minute to figure out what she said. "What trip? You going by train?" He gave her a sad smile, the sides of his mouth barely lifted. "I'll miss you, you know."

"I doubt it," she replied with more energy than he'd seen all day.

"No, I can say for certain I'll miss you." He stepped up to her and folded her in his arms. Planting a kiss on top of her autumn-colored hair, he admitted something. "I never knew my mother. But you're a good substitute." He stepped back and held her gently by both shoulders. "Now tell me about this trip. Are you going to that cattle ranch? Is some lady friend going with you?"

Melissa patted Jake's cheek. "Thank you. Yes and no."

It took Jake a second to figure out what she meant. "Yes, to the ranch but no to a friend going with you?"

"Oh, a friend all right but certainly not a lady," she chuckled. "At least the lady knight would not say so."

"I'm confused. What does Bea have to do with who's going with you?"

At that point, Melissa put both hands on her hips and got right up in his face like she did that first day. "Damn it, do you want to go to Texas with me or not?" She stomped her foot and gave him a severe frown.

To say her words shocked Jake was putting it mildly. This tiny woman was an answer to his prayers. From wide-eyed breath-holding shock to delight, Jake reached out, grabbed her around the middle and swung her around, both of them laughing like crazy people.

"We're going to Texas, woman," he yelled, his head back, joy in every word.

"Together, Jake," Melissa said, a bit out of breath but obviously happy that he'd be joining her.

"Together, lady."

"One more day, Jake." Melissa took her usual place on the stool. He sat on his bed, legs crossed at the ankles, hands crossed behind his head. "Your shoulder must feel better."

"Good enough." He uncrossed his legs and offered a hand to help her stand. "This is the last day," he said as he studied the room. "The last day for the story. We do this together, right?" For a moment, his sense of balance, of direction and purpose shuddered. But he didn't break. His story gave him an odd kind of strength. This woman he walked with gave him courage to find a new adventure.

"Together," Melissa said as she held the journal and walked with her hand tucked on Jake's arm.

Once settled, she picked up from where she left off...the moment when the soldier and the knight knew they loved each other. Today she began with them separating.

Determined to stay together, the first thing the following morning, an escort took Bea to see the women's quarters. Shortly after she left, another escort came for me.

We returned to the room, wondering why these people separated girl babies, anyone plain or disfigured from the society they'd witnessed so far.

Nowhere could we find a way to escape unless we were free to move about. Our greatest fear was that one of those lusty handsome men might try to couple with Bea. The thought terrified her and infuriated me. Couldn't we simply ask to be released? The king told us others had come to their mountain, stayed a short time then left.

When the king summoned us a short time later and told us we would be released, we were overwhelmed. Donning her armor, with her weapons and shield returned, Bea felt complete. Once again, I wore my uniform and carried my staff.

The king's favorite woman escorted us through the underground passages along with an armed escort.

'You will join the babes and children who nourish the beasts here. My advice...run!'

The door slammed shut, leaving us free but afraid we were now bait for monsters as were those left here before. Blankets and small clothing lay scattered around.

Jake laid a hand on Melissa's arm. "Wait. Wait. Please. Let me wrap my head around this." He felt sick. "How can I imagine such a horror?" He stood and waved Melissa back to the bench. These two people, as imaginary as they were, came from his mind. The soldier was Jake. He had no idea who Bea was in his world. Now that they'd gained freedom, he wasn't sure if they could win against monsters or if they could escape the mountain alive.

"When the story ended, you woke up," Melissa told him.

"Finish it," Jake said in a bitter tone. The odds of these two living at the end were small. He hoped they died with honor, had a warrior's death. That one didn't survive the other to live a half-life ever after. If they had to go, let it be together. He bowed his head and prayed the end of his story would not tear out his heart.

Roars to the left and right. The loudest from directly in front of them. Huge beautiful black and white cats—as big as a room with paws the size of an army tent. The cats backed us to the edge of a cliff—water on the far side but ragged rocks beneath the lip. No one would survive such a fall. Better to die in battle. Bea yelled a battle scream and charged forward, driving her sword into the bigger cat. I could do no less than gather my battle courage and follow her. A viscous attack injured me badly, but one swipe of a huge paw sent Bea over the cliff's edge. Insane with grief, I attacked only to sail through the air and roll over the edge myself

I can only surmise:

Two bloody pulverized bodies lay on the rocks, sword and staff close at hand. Neither one needed. Their deaths served no purpose.

Melissa stopped but didn't close the journal. She waited for Jake to control his sobs. He quietened eventually and used the sleeves of his shirt to wipe tears from his face. He didn't face her though. He turned his face to the dreary sky that looked as sorrowful as he felt.

When he said nothing, she said, "You spoke one more sentence. I'm not sure what it means. It's your story. Maybe you know."

He turned enough to look over his shoulder.

She nodded and finished his tale. *But Fate wasn't through with them yet.*

So much adventure. So much discovery and fear. So little time to truly love someone. So much courage—to face death like that.

"Together, huh, Melissa," he said sadly.

"Aye, soldier. They are together no matter where they are."

His heart hurt for the lovers who discovered each other too late. He held out a hand back toward his friend. She took it gently, and they strolled through a summer garden, far from the tragedy of death on a snowy mountain cliff. Even if only in a story.

Miles the two traveled. Sometimes they were lucky enough to catch a train on their way to St. Louis. Sometimes the tracks weren't repaired from war damage so they moved on by stagecoach.

Before Jake and Melissa left Pennsylvania, he collected his monies and purchased clothes, a Remington pistol and belt as well as a Springfield rifle along with plenty of ammunition. Traveling with an older woman meant providing protection. He carried the rifle and wore the pistol. His things went into a valise, but he carried his money on his body in case the valise went missing.

Melissa packed the things she wanted to keep in a trunk and left it with her friend, the retired professor. She carried a bigger valise than Jake's. They arrived safely in St. Louis and got hotel rooms.

"I don't know about you, but I'm gonna find a bath

house and soak until my fingers get wrinkled. You gonna order a bath for your room? You'll feel better." Jake already had clean clothes tucked under his arm.

"Looks like you've already checked on that bath house," Melissa teased him as she went through her valise. "Would you ask the desk clerk to send up a bath when you leave?"

"Sure will. Enjoy." He tipped his hat to her and gave her a wink.

"Get yourself out of here, young man," she said and laughed as she aimed a balled up towel and threw it at him. He left her laughing, a pleasant sound.

Fourteen hundred miles, give or take a hundred, found them getting off yet another stagecoach. Jake stretched his legs then turned to help Melissa down. He knew she'd suffered through all this traveling, not wanting to stop and rest. She wasn't a young person and was probably stiffer than he was. Still, she moved out, heading to the nearest hotel.

The next morning, following directions from the desk clerk, Jake rented a buckboard and slung their valises in the back. He helped Melissa up on the seat and flicked the reins over the horse's back.

They rode in silence, headed toward the ranch twenty miles west of Waco. Melissa craned her head to see the countryside while Jake kept his eyes open for anyone who might try to stop them. They'd run into men several times who refused to accept the peace agreement between the southern and northern states. Jake hadn't killed anyone, but he scared off a good many.

"The desk clerk knew Grant Stone," she said casually. "And he remembered David. Said Stone was a good man. Said David was growing into a fine man. Did well, taking care of what Stone started. He asked if David survived the war." She looked about over late summer pastures. "I told him David was gone, but my other son and I would take care of the ranch now. He seemed pleased to hear it,"

"Thanks, ma'am," was all Jake could say past the lump of gratitude blocking his throat.

They rode on, ready for a new part of their lives. Together. As it had started for them so it would continue.

Chapter Fourteen
Bea's Journey

She woke slowly, her body aching as if she'd been in one spot a long time. Her armor wrapped around her but was so bent that she had trouble moving so she could sit up. Her sword lay nearby in good condition. Her shield, however, lay in several pieces.

Unsure where she was, she looked around for the one person she expected to find. But she saw him not. "Jake?" She called for him, wondering if he was scouting this place or perhaps injured again.

When Bea tried to stand, the bends in her armor prevented it. With a sad sigh, she pulled a knife from her boot and began cutting straps and buckles. It took longer than she thought it might to remove the armor.

When at last she stood in leggings, boots and padded jacket, she worried that something had happened to Jake. He wasn't one to abandon her.

For three days, she waited. Rabbits were plentiful—these looking more like the rabbits she used to catch near her liege lord's castle.

Trying to hold in the fear that Jake was gone forever—either back to his life in 1865 or dead, she made a monumental decision. She buried her armor and shield. The pieces needed the attention of a blacksmith and were not serviceable at this time. Tears fell on each piece as she laid them with reverence in the deep hole. Each piece, serving as one, had saved her life more than once.

In their final fight, Bea thought she might have died. Did Jake die as well? She'd returned him from Death's arms once before. Sore and worn out, she filled in the hole then covered it with fallen leaves, scattering them artlessly so that even she, times from now, would not be able to locate it.

She sat with her sword finally and gave into grief, mourning Jake's loss and their love. Too late had they found each other. Resignation set in. She would find the nearest village and attempt to fit in, as a woman, rather than a knight. Her greatest punishment had come not from the mage and eight hundred years in solitude sitting on a rock. Her punishment was finding the one man she could love then losing him.

"If Jake is alive in his time, he will mourn me as well. But he will move on. Not together, he and I. But he will live his life as best he can," she told a noisy gray and white bird.

Without her armor, having only her sword and knives to protect herself, Bea left the place where she woke. Not the snowy cliff she vaguely remembered but thick woods.

Her chances of surviving in this world with over-grown killer animals was not good, but she set forth to find people. On the third day, she heard a loud noise, short and sharp. Unfamiliar with the sound she hid. Two men came through the trees, smiling and talking low.

To her surprise, she recognized their clothes. They wore pants and jackets like Jake's. Both carried a long metal stick. She wasn't familiar with that. If they did nothing else, each could serve as a staff or club.

She followed them to a deer. One bragged how he was

the best shot between the two. Quickly they cut a branch stout enough to carry the deer on. Tying it by its feet, the dead animal hung down, blood dripping from its gaping mouth. Only then did Bea realize how hungry she was. Her gut hurt. She hadn't eaten that day.

The men set off for home. She followed, wary of getting too close or making a betraying noise. Her greatest fear though was losing them. Surely, they would not be that far from where they could gut the deer and save the meat.

The two entered a clearing that expanded to hold four homes. The path they'd followed turned into a well-traveled road, wide enough to accommodate a cart. Bea hid behind brush and tree, watching. These were not her people, but Jake's. Children played near two of the homes. One child broke away from his playmates to join the men. That man, the taller one, ruffled the little one's hair and talked with him, laughing at something the child said.

Bea wasn't sure what to do next. How could she approach these people dressed as she was and carrying a sword longer than the child was tall.

Wondering if there were other homes near besides these four, she skirted the area and followed the road. She saw more and more people and at least a dozen more homes. Some kind of merchant shop sat at the far end of the road. The homes were weather worn but not in disrepair. They were bigger than any peasant home she'd ever seen.

From Jake she had learned that these kinds of places were called towns, and a law man often dispensed justice. He also said towns usually had a doctor.

He had to explain that one. "He heals folks, Bea. What do you call those men where you lived?"

"Such men are called healer."

Jake told her these men were usually kind and caring. He would trust a doctor before too many other folks.

With that goal in mind, Bea circled the town, watching for ill or injured who might lead her to the healer. She sat all afternoon waiting until finally a woman came waddling down the road. She was neither ill nor injured but instead large with child. Now and then, she would stop, lean against a cart, a fence or a tree and take deep breaths.

She approached a house near the end of town closest to Bea. Laboring against possible birth pains, she climbed the two steps to the porch and knocked. An older woman in an apron opened the door and quickly ushered her in.

All night Bea waited for the woman to leave. She waited for anyone else—like a husband—to come. But no one else came. Toward dawn when soft blue, pink and gold colors filtered into the night's inky blackness, she heard a child cry. A hearty wail from lusty lungs. The tension that tied Bea's muscles loosened, and she found tears coursing down her cheeks.

If only she and Jake... The thought died there. She might be in his world, but she had no idea of the year and certainly had no idea how to live here. Still, she would try to meet this healer and see what could happen next.

She awoke but stayed still. No man watched her but a child did. One that her kind called simple, the trip of his pink tongue sticking out slightly. Wide innocent eyes watched her without suspicion. Rather a sweet curiosity. If she moved, he might run away. Maybe this child knew the doctor? Could he take her there before the sun rose?

More importantly, why was this little one roaming the tree line alone at this time of night? A protective instinct raised its head in her heart.

No sooner did she wonder what to do next than she spotted a lantern bobbing down the road. Whoever carried it had spotted the child's white night shirt.

Bea sat still as the man drew closer but used her right

hand to push her sword in the decaying log next to her hip. She might be able to explain her clothing, boots and knives, but no one would give her time to explain if she held that particular weapon. Things were about to get awkward.

"Georgie, what are you doing out here so early. Grannie is worried. You may play outside when the sun is up, and you have eaten your breakfast." The man stooped down on one knee and gathered the boy to him in one arm.

Georgie, however, wiggled out of his grandfather's embrace and came over to Bea's side. He put a hand on her shoulder and gave the man an imploring look. As if he asked for help. For her.

Bea had heard of innocents who knew more than people often gave them credit for. Quietly she waited to see what the man might do.

"Help the lady up, boy. Grannie can visit with her while I take care of Sarah and her baby." The man stood and watched the boy who tugged on Bea's arm, attempting to help her stand. "You really do need some attention, I see." Motioning for the boy and her to follow, he led the way down the road while the little one held Bea's hand, his a small warm hand.

Up the front stairs they went and through the door into a wide space filled with chairs and lounges. Jake called them sofas.

"Run along and dress, Georgie, then go to the kitchen. Grace will have breakfast waiting." The man blew out the flame in the lantern and slid the clear globe back in place. "Miss, come with me please." He held a door opened to another section of the house. She followed him through a long hall and through another door.

This time the room changed. Benches lined the wall. A small desk stood near a door on the far side of the room. The man proceeded across the room into a short hall. He opened one door and motioned for her to enter.

She had followed him, knowing she could escape the place through any of the doors or windows she'd passed. This room, however, was small without a window. If she entered, she'd have to pass this older man to leave.

Pulling up courage, she leaned around the corner of the door without going in. Seeing such a small space, she asked, "If I enter, I may leave of my own will?"

The man looked a bit surprised but calmed. "You may." Again, he motioned her in and pulled two stools close so they could sit face to face.

Having no better plan, Bea entered and sat on one stool though she pulled it a little further back from the man.

He took a seat then studied her. He examined her features and clothing without ever touching her. Finally, he gave her a small smile that lightened his face. "What is your name, and how may I help you?"

What to tell him? This man was the village healer or as Jake would say, the town doctor. How could she explain the clothes she wore or the way she talked?

With no answer other than get to it, she tried to answer him and ask for help.

"My name is Beatrice. I am from far away. And I'm lost. Men took me and left me in the forest."

"Do you have a home?" The doctor sat with each hand atop each knee. "Do you have a husband that might be looking for you? What is your last name? We might know him, or we can help you search for him."

Bea almost cried at the man's generosity. If she were careful, she could answer his questions honestly if sparsely.

"My home is too far away to return to. My family is long gone. My husband..." Oh heavens, how to speak of Jake without crying in grief? "I think my husband followed me and was killed. His name is Jacob Border." That was true. She and Jake fought some cats—huge cats. She didn't remember if they survived the battle, but if she had to wager her life that they won, she would probably lose the wager. A bet, as Jake called it. She could hope for the best though.

Even without him at her side, his stories about life in his time were supporting her. Now she had to play this game of survival carefully.

"I am sorry for your loss, Beatrice. It appears you are stuck here. With no place to go—correct? Well, you've landed in a small community in the middle of Ohio. The nearest big city is Cincinnati." She nodded, her hands now on her knees, unconsciously mimicking him. "Have you eaten? Are you tired?"

A soft knock hit the door panel. The man must have expected such because he called out for whomever to enter. Two people came in, the child and an older woman.

"My dear, this is Beatrice." He turned to Bea then gestured to the woman. "This is my wife, Catherine. And you've met Georgie already." The little boy had already moved to Bea's side and stood with his hand on her knee.

My protector, Bea told herself. She gave the boy a smile then reached up and gently ruffled his hair as his grandfather had done. Such a beam of delight lit the little one's face. She let her hand rest on his shoulder.

"It seems as if Georgie has adopted you." The man gave her a wide grin and offered his hand saying, "I'm Doctor Lionel Hampton, at your service."

Only because Jake had shown her a handshake was she able to touch his and squeeze. That seemed to satisfy everyone.

Doctor Hampton got right down to business. "My dear, Beatrice here is without home or support. Her accent says she may not be from these shores. Would you arrange a bath and clothes? Perhaps a nightgown to start with." He turned toward Bea though he still addressed his wife. "A bath, a hot meal in her room then a few days of rest. Then I think our lady will be recovered well enough for us to help her plan her next move. Is that okay with you, Beatrice?"

"My...husband called me Bea. Please do that as it may be easier for the little one to say," she asked.

"Georgie, can you say Bea? That's her name."

The three watched the little one wallow his tongue around. After several tries, Georgie managed to say *Bea*. The doctor and his wife applauded. Bea squeezed the boy's shoulder to let him know she was proud of him.

"Come, Bea. Let's follow the doctor's orders. Bath, bed and sleep. In that order.

And as easily as that, Bea slipped into a new life, thanks to Jake's abundant stories.

"You're sick again, Bea?" Catherine held a wet washcloth to Bea's face. "I think it's time for Lionel to examine you." Catherine shooed off Georgie and supported Bea as she sat on the side of her bed in the Hampton's small attic room.

"Am I very ill, Catherine?" Bea panted as she held her queasy gut. She'd never felt so odd. Pitching up bitter bile in the morning but fully recovered by mid-day.

Catherine laughed but held out a hand to show her guest she meant no offense. "I truly believe you will no longer feel this way in about seven months."

An hour later, Bea sat on the porch, a hand over her stomach, crying soft tears. She'd upset Georgie with her tears so had to assure him she was crying happy tears. All would be well. The boy didn't quite understand, but he understood the word *happy* and her smile.

"Jake," she whispered. "I carry our child. I wish you were here. I'm scared and happy. You would be as well. I know this for true. Before I grow too large to move gracefully, I must do one more thing. I cannot leave my sword unattended. It served me well and deserves better than lying among decay in a forest." She let her gaze travel to the edge of the forest where Georgie found her. "I will do this on the morrow though how I will explain my sword to the doctor and Catherine has not come to me yet."

The next morning, Bea caught the doctor early. "Sir—" she began only to have him stop her.

"Beatrice Border, please call me Lionel. We gladly share our home and lives with you. It would honor me greatly if we were also friends."

She colored to a pale pink but gave him a smile. "I would be honored as well, sir...Lionel." They shared a bigger grin then Bea recalled what she wanted to ask him. "Lionel, my husband brought a mighty sword with him. We traveled with it and cared for it. He is gone now," That was hard for her to admit, "but I still have the sword. I left it in the forest where Georgie found me. I worry that someone may steal it or that it suffer from lack of care. Would you go with me so I can retrieve it? It must be cleaned then stored properly. And, sir, it must remain a secret, especially from Georgie. The little one does not keep secrets well."

Lionel snorted even as he laughed. "You are most delicate when you say that. The child can't keep anything to himself. By now, half the town knows the lady he found in the woods is going to have a baby." He rubbed his chin and thought a minute. "A sword you say?" She nodded, her hands twisting together in nervousness. "May I suggest we wait until well after dark this evening to retrieve it? Folks are used to seeing me out at all hours so won't think anything of it. Catherine has a dark cloak she wore when we used to travel after dark to help someone. She doesn't go with me any more since Georgie's parents died, but the cape is still in a trunk in the attic. Will that do? Tonight and a clock with a hood?"

Breathing a sigh of relief, Bea thanked him. "That will be well, Lionel."

"Best tell Catherine our plan so she can keep an eye on Georgie. He's a light sleeper as you know and tends to wander. If he sees us, he'll tell everyone."

"A thoughtful plan. I will inform her the minute Georgie is occupied." She left to find Catherine, wishing they could retrieve the sword now as she originally hoped.

The day passed slowly. Bea learned how to wash sheets and hang them to dry. She gathered towels the doctor used in his practice and washed those. She still had trouble moving in the dress Catherine found for her. Grace, the cook and housekeeper, accepted Bea because the Hamptons did but wasn't particularly friendly. She had trouble believing a grown woman didn't know how to do things like cook, do laundry, or sew. Still, the cook did help Bea learn her way around the kitchen.

The sun sank behind the trees, the night not far off. Bea paced in the front room, willing night to become as black as possible. Catherine came in leading Georgie who wanted a hug from Bea.

"Sleep well, little one," Bea said as she knelt in front of the boy and embraced him. Georgie nodded his head so hard she feared he'd break his neck.

"I'm going to read him a story and sit with him for a while. That thing you need? It's on your bed. Good luck." Leading Georgie, they mounted the stairs to the bedrooms.

As soon as they disappeared and Bea heard the door close, she gathered her skirts high and took the stairs two at a time. She snatched the cloak off her bed and returned down stairs, her feet flying. Down the quiet dark halls she went until she met Lionel in his waiting room. He carried his bag in case they met anyone.

With a practiced flourish, Bea swept the cloak out and around her shoulders.

"This isn't the first time you've done that, I'm willing to bet," Lionel said quietly.

"No and may not be the last," Bea said, conviction in her voice. "Let us retrieve the sword. I have waited long enough."

They carried no lantern. The doctor knew where he walked, and Bea had watched the spot in the woods since the day she came there. Moving quickly without running, they entered the edge of the woods where underbrush began.

Only a minute passed before Bea found the tree with the decaying log beside it. After a day's rain and several foggy mornings, she feared the sword might require more care than she could provide. Leaving Lionel to keep watch, she carefully pulled the weapon from its hiding place and slipped it within the cape's folds

"We may return to the house now," she whispered to him as she passed. They made it to the house without being seen. In one of Lionel's examining rooms, Bea moved aside her cloak and revealed the sword in the strong lantern light.

Lionel gasped. "That's the most beautiful thing I've ever seen." His mouth gaped, and his eyes widened.

Bea raised it then laid it across her body, resting the blade on her other arm. Giving Lionel a nod, she stepped forward so that he might take it. Hesitant to do so, he finally accepted it, holding it by the grip, blade upright.

He ran a hand along the edge, surprised when it drew a thin line of blood from one finger. The sharpness pleased Bea though she said nothing. Taking the sword nearer the lantern, Lionel bent down to examine the hilt.

"This is heavy though not as heavy as it looks. It must be," he stopped and took it to the table in the room. Pulling a measuring string from his coat pocket, he laid it out along the sword from the pommel, passed the grip and cross guard and along the blade to the tip. "Thirty-four inches," he said and whistled in admiration. "This belonged to a knight, correct?" Bea nodded. "A powerful one. I envy your husband. This is amazing. I see why you want to preserve it. It's a rare beauty." He turned back to her, one hand on the grip and the blade lying over his arm. "Care for it then we will find a way to protect it."

Bea accepted the sword and nodded. The weapon might never be used again, but it would always be ready.

Lionel put a hand on her arm, stopping her. "You must show this to Catherine so she is aware of such a weapon in our home. She will help find an appropriate hiding place for it."

Bea saw the wisdom of his words though she was reluctant to draw the gentle woman into her world of violence even if it only be the sight and safety of the weapon. Still, she nodded, letting Lionel know she would inform Catherine.

The blade stayed in her room, its presence a comfort to her. She borrowed a wet stone from Lionel and sharpened the edges. With a soft cloth and oil, she rubbed the blade until it glowed in the light.

Her room wasn't large but was big enough that she could practice the moves her father taught her. Moves that saved hers—and Jake's—lives many times. So much of her story remained a secret from the doctor and his wife. She regretted that, but the fewer who knew of the sword or even saw it, the better off everyone would be.

Her past was a secret—a secret being one even if only one knew it. Jake knew it, but despite the hope in her heart,

Bea feared Jake was lost to her forever. This sword was another secret she saw no reason to share with people.

Bea became a familiar sight around the small town. She was not large with child yet. Catherine encouraged her to take Georgie for walks. The boy knew no strangers. She could protect him as she learned about the people.

She admitted that her husband came from this country, a *state* called Pennsylvania but that she was a foreigner, unused to the ways here. Catherine often sat with her, telling her about the people she'd seen or those who stopped to visit because she walked with the boy.

"Like your country, I think, most people are good and hard working." Bea agreed. Catherine pointed out the other side of that though. "There are men who still resist the north winning the war. They fight in the dark. There are also those who don't want to make a living honestly in many towns. They steal or poach game from others. You must be alert at all times."

At times, Catherine would help Lionel in his practice. "Bea, would you sit at the table today and watch the waiting room?" She agreed, glad to be busy even if it was to sit with those waiting to see the doctor.

One day she sat at the small table with a roomful of town folk. One child broke his arm. A man had a deep cut on his arm. One woman thought she might be in labor. Yet another young one was bitten by a bee, and his arm was swollen. The doctor was sewing up a cut on an older man's leg, and Catherine was settling in a woman who was well into labor.

Into the waiting room rushed the woman Bea had seen her first night while hiding in the woods at the outskirts of town. "My baby can't breathe! He's trying, but he's turning blue!" the woman screamed, nodding to the child in her arms.

Knowing neither the doctor nor Catherine could leave their patients, Bea whisked the woman into the long hall leading back to the main house. She pushed the woman into a chair near the door and lifted the child from her arms.

"I have seen this before many years ago," Bea told the mother. Quickly she opened the child's mouth and looked for anything that shouldn't be there. "Do you have other children? Perhaps another young one?"

"Yes. Yes. A girl. She's two. Barely walking. A handful," the young woman wailed. Her hands twisted tightly, her fingers red from rubbing in a tangle.

Bea put her little finger in the baby's mouth. Closing her eyes, she searched and touched... Throwing off the blanket wrapped tightly around the child, she took the boy by the ankles and let him fall then jerked him up.

"What are you doing!" the mother demanded as she jumped out of her chair and tried to wrestle the baby away from Bea. She, however, was stronger and faster so with elbow and hip she avoided the mother's grasping hands as she gave the little boy two more drops and jerks.

Suddenly something flew out of the little one's mouth followed by a lusty scared wail. The mother immediately stopped fighting Bea who allowed her to scoop the baby into her arms, hugging and rocking it gently, with tears streaming down her face. Meanwhile Bea searched for and picked up a summer grape.

"Me thinks your daughter shared her food with the child, not knowing him too little to eat such," she said gently as she handed the small round grape to the mother. "Your daughter was generous." She refrained from saying her child was unwise. But then what child of two is wise in the ways of life and death. Bea could not ease the child from the mother's arm so knelt beside her and checked the little boy. "He seems to have suffered little injury though great damage to his dignity."

The mother smiled at that, a grateful happy chuckle. "A bruised dignity is okay. I'll take that as long as he lives." Bea patted her shoulder and stood, motioning her back to the waiting room.

"Best you wait here, and let the doctor check him."

The mother nodded, her eyes on her child, and sat where Bea guided her. Soon enough the serious cases received attention, and the mother with child went with Doctor Hampton for a thorough checkup.

By late afternoon, no one sat in the waiting room. Catherine brought word that the evening meal was ready. Anyone needing medical attention would check the clinic first. If closed for the day, they would come to the doctor's front door.

Lionel said grace then Catherine prepared Georgie's plate. Lionel filled a plate for Bea and passed one to his wife. After such a busy day, the adults sat quietly, resting mind and body.

When the meal ended, they gathered in the living room. George sat near Catherine, playing with blocks. He'd stack them then knock them down, making a great noise, laughing as they tumbled across the carpet.

"I checked Maria Garret's baby. He's right as rain," Lionel said.

Sudden tears sprang to Bea's eyes. Her breath hitched, and she gave one quick hiccup of a sob before regaining control.

"Bea? What's wrong, dear?" Catherine asked before Lionel could.

"*Right as rain*. Jake said that our last day together. Your words, Lionel, reminded me that I am alone now."

Lionel reached out at the same time Catherine did. Both touched her arms. "You're not alone, Bea. You have us," Lionel said sincerely. "As long as you want, you can live here with your child. If you ever leave, it will be because you want to. Not because we asked you to go," he assured her.

"Bea, every time you speak of Jake, he remains with you. Alive in your heart if not at your side. A silly phrase. A joke. A whispered word. Something you see...anything can remind you of him. Speak about those things. For certain, tell your child the stories of his mother and father. In that manner, he will live on," Catherine said.

Bea laid a hand on first Lionel's then Catherine's hand. "You are incredibly generous people. I shall never forget my sweetest Jake or you." Wiping a stray tear off her cheek, she managed to laugh. "Jake would hate to hear me call him *sweetest Jake*."

"Jacob Border, what upsets you so this day?" Bea picked up her six-month-old child and walked him as he fussed. Despite the sunny June day, the baby wouldn't settle. "Perhaps a visit with Catherine is in order." In matters of raising a child, Bea went to Catherine first.

"Catherine, Coby fusses today. He did as well yesterday. Mayhap he is ill?" Bea surrendered him to the older woman who laid the boy in her lap, his body long enough now that his feet ran up her front.

"Coby, what ails you, little one?" Catherine studied his sturdy body, pink from fussing. His cloth diaper was dry. He insisted on waving his hands around as he fussed.

"He looks so like Jake right now," Bea noted with a chuckle. "Jake rarely spoke without waving at least one hand to and fro." She demonstrated, flapping a hand up and down.

That set Catherine to laughing. "Taking after your papa, huh, little man." While the baby fussed, she stuck the tip of her little finger in the baby's mouth. "Ah, I've found the problem." She grinned at Bea as she returned the fussy baby. "This might go on for several months until all his teeth cut through. Right now, his mouth is sore, but he'll be okay soon enough." She rubbed the baby's head, ruffling thick brown hair. "Did Jake have such hair?" She led the way down the hall toward the waiting room.

"Aye, his hair grew long around his neck as we traveled. We huh..." She had to tell this carefully. "We had no way to cut his hair. When we reached a place where we could clean up, I went first. I remember returning to our room after a bath. A woman washed and braided my hair. Jake was so concerned about my safety that he didn't actually *look* at me. When he realized he hurt my feelings, he stepped back and studied me carefully. He liked what he saw. Not long after that, he too had a bath and shaved. Jake shaved himself though that seemed the job of an older man in attendance. However, the people we were with had no beard or mustache. Jake feared the man would cut them off so he risked much by taking the razor and shaving himself. He did allow the other man to trim his hair." Bea sighed as she recalled seeing Jake when he returned. He was safe, but just as importantly, that was the first time she saw him as a *man* and not a warrior or friend. "Jake's hair was this color, a light brown. Our son will look a great deal like Jake as he grows."

Once the baby was born, Catherine agreed to stay with

Georgie and Coby. Her joints grew stiff and slowed her. But she could still manage the two boys.

Bea took her place as Lionel's assistant. Some days were easier than others. Not this particular one though. They finished a rough day, and both washed their hands in the basin in his office just past the exam rooms. Lionel plopped into his padded high back chair and leaned back. Bea slumped in a small, padded chair at one side of his desk.

"Merciful heavens, I'm getting too old for this shit," Lionel confessed, his eyes closed.

Bea also sat, head back, eyes closed. "I remember one day Jake and I fought..." She snapped her mouth closed, trying to tell her story without mentioning giant butterflies but before she could finish, Lionel spoke.

"Do you realize that you do that often when speaking of Jake?"

"Do what?" Bea was so tired she had no idea to what he referred.

"You will begin a story about you two then pause for a long time before finishing. I always have the impression that how you end your stories is never quite the real ending. It does make me wonder at times what you're hiding."

"Hiding? I hide nothing," Bea replied with only a touch of heat in her words. After all, he was correct.

"You and Jake traveled but not safely. I imagine you may have been as lost as you were when you showed up here. Though what you say about Jake rings true for our times, I also have wondered where you are from and just who really owns that sword. I've seen you handle it. Your arm moves as if it is an extension. Your hand grips the hilt as if hand and hilt were forged together. That blade belongs to a knight. We have no knights in our century. I'm an old man and may be imagining this whole crazy idea, but if I were a betting man

—one who makes a wager," he amended, "I'd say you are the knight, and you and Jake traveled some nightmare place neither of you recognized."

Her mouth open in amazement, Bea managed to say, "This is an amazing tale you create, Doctor." She tried to calm her racing heart and breathe deeply enough to prevent her fainting.

"Amazing it is. And true it is as well," the doctor said, his eyes opening to slits, his hands steepled beneath his chin.

"You have listened well. Observed much. And have created my time with Jake fairly well. I will not give you details." She waved a hand at him, pushing the idea of full disclosure aside. "However, I will acknowledge that I am the blade's master. Jake and I fought for our lives several times against unbelievable animals and people. We were warriors who fought side by side. Friendship. Loyalty. Trust. Love."

She cut her gaze at him, seeing if he thought her a crazy woman. A threat to others and herself. But Lionel sat, hands steepled, his attention focused on her.

"Our last battle was not against man. Instead, we fought huge cats that circled us, slowing tearing us apart." She stopped and lifted one tired shoulder. "In truth, I know not how I survived a plunge over a cliff. I never found Jake though I searched with all my heart and soul. I searched *for* my heart and soul. He was lost to me. All I have left is his son that all may see and a sword that none may see."

Silence fell over the small room.

"I know of an abandoned barn on a farm where no one lives, not far from here. You can practice there. We may need your services someday." Lionel stood and held out a hand to help her stand. "We will not speak of this again."

Another year went by. Bea practiced with her sword several times a week, careful that no one saw her. It helped that she practiced after the sun went down. The dark cloak hid her and the sword effectively.

Rumors spread slowly through the small town. Not many had moved in after the war. Families passed through going to places like Texas, California and the great open northwest area. The demand for cattle grew after the railroads were repaired. Still, many ranchers led their cattle on long drives to places where rail cars could pick them up.

With folks passing through on their way west of Pennsylvania, the local folks started noticing items missing from their homes. Their own cows and other livestock taken. *Thieves* and *rustlers* became the topic of conversation even in the doctor's waiting room.

Bea listened to the rumors. She observed as she checked on those the doctor attended then sent home. Women close to giving birth. The elderly with serious coughs or fever. Those for whom being in their own beds was a comfort. The town wasn't big enough to have a hospital or large lie-in clinic.

"Catherine, I checked on Marian Ford this morning then Able Chance after I left Marian. Both have lost livestock. Two pigs and a milk cow. But no one has seen signs of slaughter. Perhaps these animals are being sold away from the town?" She played with the boys as she sat with Catherine after the noon meal. Soon both would lie down for a nap. While Georgie was several years older in age than her son, Georgie never objected to taking a nap.

"I was at the mercantile this morning and heard Mrs. Westerly say how they'd lost several head of cattle as well as rope and some blacksmithing tools. Wayne Westerly makes his living doing blacksmith work. He can't afford to lose tools like that."

Bea didn't say anything to Catherine but did speak to Lionel that afternoon before leaving his office. "I am going to scout around the perimeter of town tonight. I need a pair of your dark trousers and a dark shirt as well. I already have boots. I warn you now that I take the sword with me. Doing harm to these people is not acceptable." She held up a hand when he tried to speak. "I am aware of your concerns. I have not nor will I tell Catherine. But I will discover who benefits from pilfering from others."

"Take care, Bea. You are needed and loved. Discretion should be your watchword. If you are caught, you put more than your life at risk."

She nodded, aware he spoke the truth. But it was not in her nature to stand by while others suffered. Years of training rose to the top of her soul. Years of perfecting the art of war called her mind. Years of missing the other half of her very existence filled her heart and urged her to action.

For ten days, she scouted, lurking in shadows. To steal from others required darkness so she was especially vigilant during the dark of the moon. That vigilance paid off one night.

Watching the Westerly's homestead, she caught movement on the far side of the pasture. She reasoned it could be a deer but decided to check it out. Moving quietly, she positioned herself among low brush in time to see two figures ease into the pasture, slow and easy. "They do not wish to scare the cattle," she said, a whisper on the wind.

To foil the attempt, she would have to let them move out of the open field and into cover. At that point, her weapons should persuade the thieves to re-think their plans.

Using ropes as halters, the two slipped leads onto two fine looking young heifers. One went ahead of the other, letting the partner hold his lead so he could remove the loose trimmed logs that made up the pasture fence. Working efficiently but carefully, they eased the cattle out then replaced the fencing. Until the owner counted his cattle, no one would know two were missing.

Bea waited for the thieves to reach the tree line before she threw her boot knife and cut the rope holding one heifer. As quickly, she tossed the other knife. Both animals free, she threw a rock at each, scaring them into running. They blindly ran forward, knocking over one thief. Stepping into the heifers' paths, she threw up her arms and fluttered her cape, startling them into changing directions, back to their home pasture. Hopefully, they would stay close to the fence line where their companions were. She'd check on them later.

Meanwhile the two men, seeing their plan fail, set about following the cattle. Several singing swings of Bea's sword, a loud unfamiliar sound in the dark of night, dissuaded them.

Passing the trees where her knives were buried in the trunks, she followed them, hoping they'd lead her to others. To her dismay, they split up. She chose to follow the smaller man. Making his way around the town's perimeter, she stopped in shock when the man entered one of the homes. Wondering if he planned to steal something from the owner, she waited. But he never came out.

That set her to wondering. Surely, these thieves were not citizens of the town. Yet that made sense. Such men would know what to take and probably when. Sad to see that people would rob from their own, she returned to the Westerly's pasture. If she returned the cattle to the pasture, no one would realize an attempted robbery. If, however, the two animals were out but nearby perhaps suspicions would be raised and precautions set in place.

She set herself to watching the heifers for the rest of the night. Thankfully neither moved far from the flower garden in Mrs. Westerly's front yard.

"Who lives at the north end of town in the brown house," Bea asked the next morning at breakfast.

"Sam Thompson and his son. His wife left him shortly before you arrived," Catherine supplied as she poured another cup of coffee. "Why?"

"I have seen him several times when out walking, but he seems not a hospitable man," Bea said as she cut bread and butter into smaller pieces for Coby.

No one mentioned the man again. But Lionel cut his eyes toward Bea when Catherine wasn't looking. She gave him a slight nod.

"You're sure that was Thompson?" Lionel asked when they were alone an hour later. "He's surly and not bright. He and his son work on a small farm west of here for a man named Gordon. You didn't see the other man though?"

"No. I could only follow one when they split up. Does this Thompson have a friend? One perhaps taller than him?"

"I don't know, Bea." He held up his hands and shrugged both shoulders. "When you go out next, maybe you'll run into them again."

Two nights later, when the moon was a sliver in the night sky, Bea found the two again near a farm on the outskirts of town. This time the two had their eye on a horse. Bea knew the owner and also knew his prize draft horse stayed in a stable in the barn at night rather than an open pasture.

Again, the two men moved confidently but cautiously to the barn then slipped inside. Bea used the small door at the other end of the barn to enter. The weak moonlight outside did not penetrate into the barn. All to her advantage. Pulling out her sword, she eased up beside the stall. Thompson was looking for a halter for the big horse. He found one and turned to walk back to his partner's side, but one swoosh of Bea's sword cut the halter in two. Thompson stood with mouth hanging open, looking at the pieces of the harness in his hand and on the ground. Clearly, he was confused as he called for his partner.

"Gus? Gus, get over here. Something...something happened." He held up the harness for the other to see.

In the dark, wearing dark clothes and wrapped in a black cloak, Bea was invisible. So much so that she stood two feet behind Thompson with neither man the wiser.

The partner gave a funny squeak, thumped Thompson, and cussed him in disgust. "You idiot! You must have picked up a broken halter."

"But Gus, I didn't. I heard a sound, and something flew through the air then I saw this...cut in half." Thompson whined like a kid.

"Now I'll have to find some rope and put it around this big fellow's neck in order to lead him out of here." Gus searched the front of several stalls until he found a coiled-up rope. Gathering it and headed to the horse's stall, he squeaked again when a swishing sound came from his right, and the rope disintegrated into several pieces at his feet. Another swish and his hat sailed off his head.

"Thompson, I swear if you're trying to be funny, it ain't working," Gus whispered, his voice tense with nerves.

"Funny? Ain't nothing funny about tonight," came the other man's frightened surprise.

"We gotta get this horse out of here. That wagon master said he'd pay double if we brought it tonight. Those wagons are pulling out before dawn. Ain't no one gonna suspect the animal's missing till Warren comes out to get him after breakfast."

"Maybe this ain't such a good idea," Thompson observed.

Bea agreed. So far, the two were scared but not enough to stop them.

The taller man took a step forward, intent on opening the stall door. Suddenly he screamed as a knife pinned his hand to the wood. Thompson was behind him and jumped when his partner screamed. Something touched the man's arm, something soft and glowing. This time it was Thompson screaming.

"We gotta get out of here, Gus. There's ghost in here. One just touched me."

"Help me! I can't get this knife out of my hand. It's buried deep." Gus yanked Thompson to his side, and together the two managed to pull the knife out. Gus threw it on the barn floor practically at her feet. She snatched it up before either one of them thought to keep it

"Let's get out of here. We can sell this big devil later. Right now, I gotta get to Doc Hampton. My hand is bleeding bad, and it hurts like hell," Gus complained. Both men left the barn and made it into the woods.

Assured the horse was all right, Bea followed them, but they'd disappeared into the dense forest that bordered the place.

"Not a problem," Bea said as she cleaned blood from her knife in the stream. "I believe we will see you at the doctor's place soon."

She made it to the house, threw off the dark clothes and cloak as soon as she could. Slipping on her nightgown and dressing robe, she gave her knife a quick cleaning and made sure her sword was all right. It had only cut a halter and rope that night, but a soldier could never take a weapon for granted.

Planting herself at the kitchen table with a glass of milk, she waited for the man named Gus to show up. Twenty minutes passed before he came knocking on the front door.

"Rather an urgent pounding." Bea grinned as she left the kitchen.

She answered the door and ushered the man into the waiting room, telling him to wait there while she fetched Doctor Hampton, that he alone had the key to the exam rooms and office.

"I sleep lightly these days, especially when I know you're out there. Who is here at this time of night?" Lionel wore his night robe, cinched at the waist, his hair only finger combed. "Have you been to bed?"

"I arrived home not long ago. Your patient is in the waiting room. He seems to be in considerable pain." She refrained from smiling. She didn't want the doctor knowing how the man was injured just yet.

"Let's take care of him then." Lionel led the way down the hall and greeted the man before moving him quickly into an examining room. The man had wrapped a cloth around his hand, but blood seeped out onto the floor.

"This is a nasty wound, sir. How did you come by it?" Lionel turned the hand one way then another, holding it over a clean towel.

"I'd rather not say, Doc. I got into a disagreement with someone and got this for my trouble. Will my hand be okay, you think?"

"Your name, please. Mrs. Border must enter it in my log book before she can help me set this hand to right."

"Gus. Gus Turner. I'm camped out north of town. Been meaning to come in and find a job. This little town's on the road that folks travel when they're headed west. I figure I can help someone here or maybe hook up with folks headed out."

Bea dutifully made note of Gus Turner and his condition before returning the logbook to Lionel's office. Then she donned a heavy apron over her nightclothes and helped the doctor.

Sometime later, Lionel bandaged the hand and sat back, a frown marring his face. "Mr. Turner, I have to be honest. I'm not sure if your hand will ever work properly again. If you let it heal then exercise it, you may get function back. I've done my best." He stood and motioned for the patient to head toward the waiting room. Along the way, he told Gus Turner what his fee was for the surgical work he did, trying to repair a badly injured hand.

"I can't pay you all at once, Doc. I ain't got a steady job yet, but I'll bring what I can later today. I figure I need some rest right now." He turned the front doorknob and left without another word.

"He does look poorly, Bea. I'd hate to be the man who stabbed his hand like that. Not only did that knife cut muscle but severed tendons that may never heal correctly." Lionel shook his head as he mounted the first step to return to bed. "If you haven't gotten any sleep yet," he began as he turned to look at her over his shoulder. To his surprise, Bea stood at the bottom of the staircase, a wide grin on her face and a twinkle he'd never seen in her eyes.

"Oh! Oh, you didn't!" He padded back down the stairs to stop in front of her. She hadn't used up that smug smile yet. "You did that?" When she gave him a slow noble nod, he stuck his hands in his pocket, his face wearing a dumbfounded expression. "Well, I'll be damned. No wonder he didn't want to talk about the situation. But, Bea, you'll have to be extra careful now. He may not know who or how, but he's aware something odd is going on."

"Worry not, Lionel. If he and his partner persist in this foolishness, he will pay the price." Bea lost her smile as she spoke. A knight stood before the doctor; he just didn't know it.

The thefts stopped. Bea reasoned that Gus wasn't able to use his hand yet and his partner, the smaller Thompson, wasn't capable of doing the jobs alone.

She scouted his camp several times when she saw him enter the small tavern. Nothing hid there that shouldn't be there. Having dealt with foolish knaves in her time, she knew the two would not be able to resist robbing again. Especially since it seemed the robberies had stopped.

Gus Turner returned to Lionel's office twice. Once to pay him a paltry amount of money toward his bill and a second time a month later to let the doctor check the hand.

"His hand does poorly, Bea. It's almost healed, but he can't grasp and hold small items. His fourth finger barely bends. He is *not* a happy man. With the hand being all it can be now, I suspect he'll either move on or return to robbing folks hereabouts." Lionel shook his head and returned to deal with his next patient.

Neither had said a word to Catherine about Bea locating the robbers or her injuring one.

Wishing Gus would leave town, Bea discovered one night that the two had made off with several farm tools the owner left outside. She'd noticed that folks became lax about taking care of their property when they thought the problem had cleared up. She snorted, thinking what fools people were no matter when they lived. Eight hundred years ago she'd seen the same thing often enough.

Determined to rid the town of these two, she focused on Daniel Thompson's house. Several nights later she saw Thompson sneak out of his house well after midnight. He led her through thick woods to the southern side of town. Together the men moved close to the Vanderland's home.

Sarah Vanderland told Catherine that she and Samuel were going to visit her sister in Harrisburg. Mr. Vanderland came from a wealthy family. He and his wife had no children so were free to move away from Harrisburg. The man owned the mercantile and traveled often, setting up other places along the route west. Catherine often said she suspected they too would move further toward St. Louis as his stores grew.

Bea knew the Vanderlands. The wife was delicate with quiet graces. The husband, however, reminded her of several men who had lived in her liege lord's kingdom. Always interested in money, often at the expense of others. Such men often had grand schemes that should make them appear heroic or well-known. Rarely did such schemes work, and when each failed, those inconsiderate, often greedy men found someone else to blame.

Up onto the porch Bea went, stalking the two would-be robbers. Not if she could help it, she vowed. Caution moved to the front of her mind though. Trapped inside the house with these two wasn't good even though no one was home. Up the men went, searching the rooms at the top of the stairs. Gus called to Daniel when he found the room he wanted. Bea eased up the stairs, working on an idea that should trap the two with their loot inside the house. What she didn't count on was Samuel Vanderland standing at the bottom of the staircase, antique pistol in hand.

Good God, the man would only have one shot. He didn't even have a revolver. What was he thinking? That these two would stand by calmly while facing a one-shot pistol?

When the action came, Bea had to move with as much stealth as possible. Vanderland didn't make it easy. He planted himself at the bottom of the stairs, but Gus had no intentions of stopping. When Vanderland's pistol went off,

Gus ducked, and Thompson caught the shot right through the head. He immediately pitched forward, distracting Vanderland. Gus took the moment to toss the man against the wall. Thompson and Vanderland lay in a pile at the bottom of the staircase.

Bea threw herself over the upstairs banister and landed beside the crumpled men. Her head buried deep in her hood in a dark house, she faced Gus as he practically impaled his body on her sword. Grasping the baluster, he made a quick turn and headed back the way he came. He didn't get the bedroom door fully closed before a booted foot kicked it opened again. Backing up, almost jabbering in fear, he eased his way across the room, his eyes locked on the two hands wrapped around a silver sword's hilt.

"What the hell are you!" he screamed even as he picked up a wooden rod probably intended for hanging curtains that lay folded on a bench near the window. With the rod in hand, he turned it so it now resembled a staff. He gathered courage and ran at her. At the last minute, he switched the rod to a cane, intent on bashing in his attacker's head. He managed to strike a blow but also turned himself back into the room rather than out the door. He attacked again to the point where Bea was forced to fight him for real. Her goal was to incapacitate him and leave him there for the authorities to find. With Vanderland down and possible dead along with Thompson who was definitely dead, Gus Turner was all she had right now.

In the end, it was as fools often do. They are the makers of their own undoing. After attacking Bea's sword, Gus stepped back as if exhausted. Bea watched him, but in the dark, she couldn't see his eyes. He surprised her, rushing headlong at her. At the last instance, she raised her sword to defend, but he ran straight into her, the sword buried in his chest to the hilt. He collapsed to the floor. The sword remained in Bea's sturdy grip, the blade sliding out as he fell.

Bea quickly pulled off one glove and bent down to check for a pulse as Lionel had taught her. None. The man was dead. His partner was dead. She wasn't sure about Thompson, but Gus had a pocket of Mrs. Vanderland's jewelry. The reign of thefts in the town was ended.

At that point, Bea realized in the few minutes between the shot, Thompson's death and Gus's, others had heard and were approaching the house. Best she disappeared. Though the window was blocked by a piece of furniture and a pile of fabric, Bea eased the window opened, stepped out onto the roof, and climbed up until she was on the far side of the house from those running. She made her way across the roof then down a trellis before crouching low and angling toward the forest.

Lionel was called to exam the bodies. Catherine remained at the house. The boys slept peacefully so Bea, back in a dress and shawl, accompanied the doctor.

Vanderland was alive but suffered a head wound. He was unconscious.

"Best contact his wife. I believe she is staying with her sister in Harrisburg. My wife will know where. We can do that in the morning." Lionel nodded to several men who carried the patient to the doctor's office. One room could be used by a bed-bound patient if needed. "I shall be right behind you," Lionel told the litter bearers. "I'll certify these deaths first."

"No need to spend time on Thompson," Lionel told the city major. "It appears that Vanderland used that ancient pistol and shot him as he came down the stairs. The man's pockets are stuffed with money and jewelry." He waved the men forward who would carry the body to the stable where the stable keeper who served as an undertaker would prepare a pine coffin. "Someone go to Thompson's home and tell his son please."

Bea and Lionel followed another man upstairs and into the main bedroom. The room lay in disarray. In the midst of the distraction lay the man with the maimed hand, Gus Turner. He laid on his back, eyes wide even in death.

"Looks like he seen a ghost," the man with them said with a shudder.

"Mayhaps, he did," Bea observed with a lifted brow that only Lionel saw.

"I've never seen a wound like that, Doc." The man pointed to the slender wound. "What could do that?" The man rocked from foot to foot, wiping his hands on his pants.

"A long knife could do this, but no one in this town that I know of has such a thing. He's dead with a pocket of stolen goods. Leave all that here. Mrs. Vanderland can tell us if anything else is missing when she returns. In the meantime, I suggest a guard be posted here so no one else attempts to take advantage of the situation."

"Will do, Doc." The man couldn't leave the room fast enough.

"Best we get back to my office and open up for Vanderland," Lionel said. Making sure no one was around, he nodded to Bea. "Well done."

In 1873, a cholera epidemic took out one-third of the town. Bea and Lionel worked tirelessly, but no matter what they did, they were unable to save Catherine and Georgie. Coby became ill but survived—barely.

Worn out from constant work and little or no rest, Lionel succumbed. In a matter of two short months the disease came, decimated then vanished, leaving households without mothers, fathers, brothers, sisters, or elders.

Bea finally collapsed at the end of a week when she found no one ill. Only then did she gather her child to her, lay down, and sleep.

The bodies had to be burned so no graves marked the family who had taken her in. She and Coby worked together to carve a wooden plague to be erected in the town's cemetery. On it were the names of Dr. Lionel and Catherine Hampton as well as Georgie Grover. They dug a place to stand it up in a corner of the cemetery, beneath an oak, like the one where Georgie found Bea. Once folks saw what she and her son did, the sounds of woodcarving rang through the town for several days. On Sunday, the families walked together to the cemetery and placed the memorial carvings in three long lines beside the Hampton's marker.

Bea watched the faces of those she had come to know, admire, and respect. A body could stand only so much grief. This place had given her one precious thing but robbed her of so many others: Jake, Georgie, Catherine, and Lionel. She watched her eight-year-old son mingle with others. He too had lost so many playmates and the boy whom he grew up with, his adopted brother as Coby called Georgie. She made a decision, but she had to discuss it with her son.

On the front porch that late winter day, she pulled her tall son on to her lap. She brushed his hair off his forehead, remembering the time when his father lay near death as did his son not long ago.

"Coby, I have given thought to moving on. Moving west. I find little reason to stay here. Those we love are gone. Your father..." She tried to say what was in her heart without sounding odd. "He always talked of going to Texas and working with cattle."

Coby knew all about Jake. Bea made certain to tell him

stories of them meeting and traveling together. When he was little, she turned their adventures into bedtime stories. His favorite one was the time Bea and Jake had a contest to see which could bring in the most rabbits. Though the boy knew them as tales, she knew them as the truth.

"Texas is a long ways from here, Mother. Can we make it? Do we have money for that kind of trip?" He sat on her lap, his brown eyes focused on her, waiting for answers.

"You look so like Jake sitting like that, you know?" She patted his back and addressed his concerns. "Lionel gave me money over the years. *Pay* he called it for helping him and these people." She gestured out toward the town. "So yes, we can afford to travel though we should be careful how and where we spend that money."

"The trip is a long one. I spoke of traveling with Catherine many times, but she always found valid reasons for staying." Bea gave Coby a mischievous grin and a wink. "She was a sly one, was your Granny Catherine."

"But Granny and Granddad Lionel weren't my real kin, were they? Not Georgie either." Coby sat up. He still missed them.

"Those three were family of the heart, sweet boy, and do not you ever forget that," Bea said as she tickled him. "We can be sad and miss them. But they go with us here when we travel." She laid a hand over his heart.

"So, the question I put to you, young man, is this: do we go to Texas or not?"

For a long minute, Coby thought. He got up from her lap and went to the porch rail where he braced his hands and gazed over the landscape, with a few patches of snow still tucked into corners but the heads of flowers beginning to break through.

"Yes, ma'am. It's time to move on. Find an adventure and live it," he declared.

Bea joined him at the rail, her eyes bright with unshed tears. "Young warrior, you have your father's heart. I never knew what happened to him." She let her gaze fall on Coby. "This you know. I can only hope he did not suffer in death, or if he lived, that someday we might find him." She shrugged. "Either way, we plan then go. I have something to pack..."

"Your sword?"

"How do you know of this?" She turned him to her, her heart racing. "Tell me!" she demanded.

"A few years back, I was in the woods. You and Granddad were out all night with a patient. I thought you'd gone to bed, but I found an old barn. I started to go inside and explore, but I heard grunts and shouts. Not real loud but then I was standing right outside the small door. I managed to wiggle in through a busted slat in a stall, and there you were in a long shirt and pants. It was amazing watching you." His eyes sparkled as he told his story, his focus on that day, not her.

"Why did you not tell me?"

"I told Granddad. He'd never seen you with your blade, but he'd known about the sword long before I was born. So we sneaked to the barn a few times at night and watched you, especially when the moon was full and fell across the floor through holes in the roof. You were magic, Mother. But it was your magic and not to be shared."

He spoke so solemnly that he impressed Bea. She pulled him to her and gave him a bear hug, strong enough to make him grunt. "I love you, sneaky boy that you are," she laughed as she kissed his forehead.

"When can we start packing? Clothes, money, our guns and rifles, ammo. And food! Can't forget food!"

"I will wrap the sword first and send it to Catherine's

cousin Violet in St. Louis. Then we will collect our things and begin our new adventure."

"Mother?"

"Yes?"

"I think Granddad, Granny Catherine, and Georgie would be happy for us."

"I think you are surely right, my son."

Chapter Fifteen

Late Summer 1873

"Boss, you sure this is a good idea?" Valdez sat his horse, needing reassurance that carrying that much money was a wise idea.

"Maybe not a *good* idea but this is the only way from here to Ft. Worth. I want to buy that herd before Magellan gets his hands on it. It's not safe to send that much money by stagecoach or rail. We've got enough men, and we'll be riding fast. We don't have to stick to roads or trails. Damn few know what we're planning though I thought I saw one of Magellan's men in town the other day."

Valdez scratched his chin. "We might make twenty-five miles a day, figuring less than a hundred miles from here to Ft. Worth. Maybe four days if we have no trouble."

"Sounds about right. We'll head out at day break." Jake Border slapped his hat against his leg to knock the dust off. Like his foreman Valdez, he wasn't sure if this was a smart idea or not, but he had an itch at the back of his neck that meant getting this money to Ft. Worth might best be done on the sly.

Marcus Magellan showed up as if by magic two years earlier, about the time Jake lost his partner. Since then

Magellan had done everything possible to buy off Jake, shut him down or even kill him. The man plain didn't like him for some reason.

Jake went in the house, washing up for supper. Luz had left a steak, fried potatoes, and a slice of cake for him before going home to Valdez. They'd been here when he arrived eight years ago, and he valued both more and more each day.

As the sun set, the sound of cattle in the far pasture calmed. Rain clouds were forming on the western horizon. He hoped any storm would pass by tonight and wring itself out before dawn. He disliked riding in rain.

Rain hammered the house for several hours right after dark. Jake sat on the deep porch with a cup of coffee and watched lightening play across the sky. He didn't like riding in rain though working cattle in a much-needed rain never bothered him. Eventually the clouds blew off to the southeast, leaving behind a fresh-washed scent of earth. From under the eve of the porch emerged a large black and orange butterfly. Jake sat still, letting it explore around him before taking off for the far end of the porch.

Memories flashed through his mind. After so many years, he still questioned if they came from something real or from the story he'd once told an old woman who wrote it all down. He *remembered* fighting a huge butterfly with a woman who wore metal armor and carried a deadly sword.

Sometimes at night, he'd dream things that the old woman hadn't written down. In the light of day, he always told himself he'd not said that part aloud as he wrestled injuries and fever. Or he'd shake his head and say, "She didn't hear me right. She forgot to write *that* down." Even now, he refused to believe the story in that journal actually happened because if it were all true...

He sighed and stretched. The night was moving on, and he needed some rest before leaving. He settled into a wide lonely bed and admitted: if that story was real then he'd met and lost someone he loved. That thought alone made Jake say the story was just that, something from a fevered mind.

Dawn sat just below the horizon when Jake stepped out onto the porch the next morning. He hadn't slept well but from anxiety about this ride or illusive dreams about a brown haired, gray-eyed woman he wasn't sure. He slipped a full saddlebag off his shoulder and left it on a chair. He leaned his Springfield rifle against the wall. Going down the steps, he leaned down to pick a handful of flowers that Luz grew there. Bunching them in one hand, he rounded the corner of the house and angled for a stand of oaks about a hundred feet away. Inside the trees was a simple cemetery. The man who started the ranch, Grant Stone, was buried there. A stone marker carried the name David Woods, Stone's young partner, who died in the war. Beside that marker lay Jake's partner and David's grandmother, Melissa Woods.

Jake missed her as much as he missed the woman in his dreams. If not for Melissa, he'd never have that journal where she wrote down all he said while ill. If not for Melissa, he had no idea where he'd be now. She saved him when she asked him to come to Texas with her and help run David's cattle ranch that she inherited.

"Hey there, Melissa." He knelt and laid the flowers on the grass. "I'm setting off on one of those adventures we're always talking about, partner. I'm not so sure about this one. I got a funny feeling things could go wrong. Then again how many times did we say that and things turned out better than we ever imagined?" He looked around, hoping he'd live to come back and tell her what happened.

Leaving the small cemetery, he returned to the porch, gathered his things, and mounted the horse that Valdez brought up from the stable for him. Luz stepped up to Valdez' side. He bent down and kissed her, which got the two other men to hooting. The couple ignored them. Luz finally left her husband's side and paused beside Jake's horse. "Vaya con dios, Boss."

With her blessing, Jake nodded once then reined his horse around, headed to Ft. Worth. They trotted then walked the horses. Trotted some more, taking care to stop for water and food, letting the horses rest as well.

That night found them deep in a grove of oaks. They kept the fire low. After a long day, it felt good to sit still. Martin and John turned in shortly after full sunset. Valdez sat near Jake a while longer, talking about the cattle they wanted to get with the money they carried. Finally, Valdez turned in, leaving Jake to sit alone watching the flames dance. In an idle moment, he glanced across the fire, expecting to see...

"Damn!" Disgusted with himself at wishful thinking, he rolled over in his bedroll. As he drifted off to sleep, he imagined he saw a knight sitting across from him. Men don't cry, he reminded himself as a single hot tear slipped from the corner of his eye to fall on his hand.

Dawn saw the fire doused after a fast meal of beans and hot coffee. The four set off again. At one point, their path would intersect the stagecoach road. They wouldn't ride that road. Being taken for robbers wasn't part of anyone's plans. But they'd ride parallel to it.

Martin rode behind them, not as visible as the others. His job was to watch for anyone following them. He surprised Jake when he pulled up beside him shortly after they finished the noon meal and rode out again.

"Boss, someone's following. This ain't the first time this guy's done tracking either. I can tell. He's being careful that no one sees him."

"Bet he doesn't know you're as good as him, huh?" Jake put spur to his horse's side, picking up the pace. "Fall back, and keep your eye open." With a nod, Martin slowed his horse so the others would outdistance him.

Jake motioned for them to move closer to the coach road. They'd worry about someone thinking them robbers if they had to. Right now, he was more worried about being bottled up in a defenseless place. The coach road at this point ran along some rough terrain. Rough enough to give them cover if necessary.

They hadn't gone far before they heard the sound of multiple gunshots. The four riders stopped and waited for what might come next. A woman's scream set them in motion, galloping fast to the road.

At least two dozen men surrounded a stagecoach. The outrider and driver lay dead on the coach roof. Two men, a child and someone in a long, hooded cloak stood outside the coach.

"What are they waiting for, Boss," Martin asked as the four sat inside the tree line. Jake shook his head. He'd never seen a situation quite like this one. Stagecoach robbers took valuables as quickly as possible. Depending on their morals, they might wear covers on their faces and leave the passengers unharmed as long as no one did anything stupid like trying to shoot one of them. Other robbers worked as quickly but didn't cover their faces or leave survivors. He wasn't sure about this bunch.

A gunshot rang out but not from the men by the stage or a passenger. Jake searched the area and finally spotted the person responsible. "Damn, it's Magellan. What's he playing at?"

He no sooner said that than Marcus Magellan stood tall and prominent on a boulder on the other side of the stage. "Show yourself, Jake Border! Give me what I want, and these people can go on their way."

Jake refused to answer. His ranch depended on getting this money to the bank. His nervousness set his horse to prancing, sensing his rider's emotion.

"Come out now, or one of them dies," Magellan called out. "Abner, grab the kid." A man stepped forward and reached out for the boy, but the mother screamed, bent, and threw in one easy motion. The man reaching for the boy laid dead, a knife in his throat.

"Grab her!" Men swarmed toward her. She fought, but one managed to restrain her hands in a strong grip. Meanwhile the boy turned into a demon, attacking the men.

"This can't go on. Magellan will kill them. You three stay here. I'll go." Jake carried the money. He almost tossed it to Valdez but knew the other man would kill them all if Jake couldn't produce the money.

He turned the horse to the road and left the cover of the trees. One hand on the reins and the other in the air, he rode in slowly. The male passengers were older men, one sickly looking. They'd be no help if a firefight broke out.

Magellan remained in the rock, his rifle tucked into his arm, ready to gun down Jake. Only when Jake stopped and stepped down on to the hard packed road did Magellan relax enough to come down, his rifle held low.

Suddenly all hell broke loose. The man holding the woman gagged as her elbow crushed his neck. Like the wind, she swung the boy into the coach, and he tossed a rifle to her. She took a knee and began pumping lead into the attackers. Jake managed to grab his rifle from the scabbard and shoo the animal out of harm's way. The older men hunkered under the coach, a dangerous place to be if the well-trained coach horses panicked.

From the coach Jake heard gunfire, a pistol. What the hell? Was that the kid? From the tree line where he left his men came rifle fire. His men helped, but these attackers weren't average cowboys but trained fighters. Probably former military men. And they outnumbered Jake, his men, the woman, and boy.

She figured that out as well. "Cover me!" she called out as she headed for rocks beside the road. Jake laid down fire but saw quickly that his shots had little effect. He needed to get to higher ground along the ridge that hugged the road. His men were in a good position but, like him, not high enough to draw down on this crew.

Once she made the rocks, bullets bounced off so close to her that chips flew. Still, she clawed for higher ground. "Cover!" she called again.

Jake wasn't sure if his men could hear her. Their fire didn't increase. He was the only one who could help. Gunfire rang out consistently. He wasn't sure how much ammunition the woman or the kid had.

"Hey kid, you got enough ammo?"

"Yes sir! Help my mother. She's a damn good shot, but she needs help."

"Watch the language, kid. I'm trying to help," Jake called.

He scanned the area, trying to find a good path to take. He hoped the woman wasn't foolhardy enough to attack on her own. His military training served him well. Before he could try to lead her by voice, the sound of gun and rifle fire slacked for several seconds. Through the smoke of gunfire, Jake heard a call that sent shivers down his back, set his heart to pounding, and his soul to singing.

"Warrior, to me!"

She called to him as she moved. Exactly as he'd planned. But this woman led the way. Jake could do no less than follow her and pray his imagination wasn't playing games with him.

"Lead on. I'm right behind you," he bellowed as gunfire broke out again, men moving to get a better shot at the two. More of the attackers went down.

Magellan stayed in the fight, safe behind three of his men. He swung his rifle up to shot at the woman, but Jake took out one of his men, the dead man bumping into Magellan, messing up his shot.

The woman finally gained high ground but grunted when a bullet hit her shoulder. "Tis a flesh wound, Warrior," she yelled at Jake as he came up beside her. Seeking a better spot, she moved higher. Between her, Jake, the kid in the coach and Jake's men in the trees, the attackers' numbers dwindled until only Magellan and one man remained. The kid took out that man, leaving Magellan alone, blood running down one leg and dripping from a head wound.

Guns and rifles trained on him, the survivors slowly gathered at the coach. Jake's men led the horses down. The boy climbed out and made his way to his mother, his pistol up, moving sideways, never taking his eyes off Magellan.

When they gathered, the woman still wore the hood up. As much as Jake wanted to confront her, he had unfinished business with Magellan.

Safe with her boy, the woman kept her rifle aimed at him but gasped. "How are you alive, mage? You should have died eight hundred years ago!" she screamed and started for him.

"Dishonored knight, this time you die!" he bellowed and flung out his hands. Whether to shot her or use magic Jake didn't know and never would. Valdez wasn't waiting around to find out what Magellan planned to do.

A rifle shot rang out. A red hole blossomed in Magellan's forehead. Slowly the man crumbled to the ground, dust flying up around him. He lay in an ugly tangle of arms and legs, as ugly in death as his intentions in life.

For a full minute, everyone stood, frozen in relief that they still lived. The boy broke the moment when he flung his arms around his mother. She hugged him tightly, her cloak covering him as hers had covered Jake so far back in time that it seemed impossible.

"Bea?" That's all he could say. Tears streamed down his face, leaving muddy streaks on cheeks and chin. He dared not hope. But no one had called him *Warrior* in so long. Not since he lost her on that cliff.

He couldn't move, afraid. What if this woman wasn't the one who owned his heart? "Bea? Please?"

She set her son to one side and must have given the boy a smile. Perhaps said sometime because the boy cut his eyes shyly toward Jake and gave him a timid smile.

"Do you still love me, Warrior?" the woman asked as she pulled back the deep hood to reveal her face. "I have loved you since the day we learned to love. I have seen your face for eight years in our son. He is very much like his father, a warrior in his own right."

Unlike Jake, who couldn't move a muscle though belief spread across his face at the sight of hers, she came to him, folding her arms around his neck and pulling his lips to hers. Together they cried, lost to the men who watched but not to the child they gathered into the circle of their love.

"Warrior, to me" served them well for the rest of their days, knowing Time had pulled them apart, but Fate had reunited them.

THANK YOU FOR READING

Did you enjoy this book?

We invite you to leave a review at your favorite book site, such as Goodreads, Amazon, Barnes & Noble, etc.

DID YOU KNOW THAT LEAVING A REVIEW...

- Helps other readers find books they may enjoy.
- Gives you a chance to let your voice be heard.
- Gives authors recognition for their hard work.
- Doesn't have to be long. A sentence or two about why you liked the book will do.

About the Author

I'd like to think that I am a well-rounded person: wife, mother, educator, volunteer, quilter, and writer. Through all of these activities, my passion has always been writing. Practice makes each story better. A love of what you're writing works wonders for your attitude though I can't always say it does wonders for housework, laundry, or cooking. I want readers to enjoy what I present. If I can write a story like that then I will leave a satisfying legacy behind.

jr-carver.com

Also by Jane Carver

With Satin Romance

Return With Honor

The Answer Key

The Long Winding Road

The Sergeant and the Knight

With Melange Books

Forever Changed

The Gilpin Girls

Writing as Jane Grace
with Fire & Ice Young Adult Books

Until I'm Safe

Ghosts In My Soul

www.ingramcontent.com/pod-product-compliance
Lightning Source LLC
LaVergne TN
LVHW090603110826
845146LV00001B/240

* 9 7 9 8 8 8 6 5 3 4 6 5 8 *